BITTER END

NASHVILLE IMMORTALS BOOK ONE

BITTER END

SHAUNA JARED

For Jeff and Gunnar, thanks for putting up with me. I love you both so much!

To all my alpha and beta readers, thank you for your invaluable feedback and support.

Table of Contents

Chapter 1

"I am so screwed."

I folded my arms on the bar and dropped my head to rest on them. Joey, the bartender, mercifully poured another shot of vodka and nudged my elbow with it. I looked up, gave him a thankful smile and downed the shot. Joey gave me a sympathetic look.

"Come on Cricket, you hated that job anyway. It's a blessing in disguise." He poured another generous helping of vodka into the shot glass and passed it back to me. I was feeling the effects of the alcohol, but I was also still feeling the embarrassment of losing my job, so I kept on drinking.

The Rusty Nail in downtown Nashville had become my favorite after work spot and the bartender, Joey Morley, with his shaggy, dark brown hair, deep brown eyes, and muscular build was not hard to look at. I checked him out now in my inebriated state as he wiped the bar down. I admired his bulging biceps peeking out beneath the tight white t-shirt he wore. He was tempting alright, but Joey had become one of my best friends. He knew all about my job, my teenage daughter who had recently gone goth and vegan, my grandma, Betty, who lived in the other side of the duplex I lived in, and Grandma's new boyfriend, Gus, who was eighty-two and still had all his equipment in working order, according to Grandma. Eww. It occurred to me just then that maybe Joey knew too much. But I'd think about that when I was sober. Right now, all I could think about was the fact that I was now unemployed and in need of another drink.

"You're absolutely right, Joey." I slammed the shot glass onto the bar. "Screw the law firm of Abernathy, Smith, and Sanchez. They are exactly what their initials spell... Especially Sanchez!"

I was growing louder in my denouncement of ASS, my former employer as of this afternoon. I mean seriously, had none of those obnoxious pricks stopped to think about their acronym? I noticed through the smokey haze inside the bar that the other bar patrons were looking my way with judgmental stares. Joey was looking a little worried as well, I noted, as he returned the nearly empty bottle of vodka to the shelf.

"Bless your heart, what happened, honey?" I looked up to where the sweet southern accent was coming from. A woman, maybe in her mid-50s, was sitting at the end of the bar and apparently had heard my diatribe. She had shoulder length curly blonde hair teased with bangs which looked like the 80s had called and wanted their hairstyle back. Blue eyeshadow and pale pink lipstick paired with skintight black leather pants and a leopard print blouse, cut to reveal her ample bosom, finished her look. All she needed was a pair of jelly shoes to complete the 80s look, I thought. However, she seemed genuinely concerned about my plight, judging from her expression as she vaped Tutti Frutti, which was printed on the package she discarded.

Joey had moved down the bar to attend to other customers, so that left me with Farrah Fawcett, who was now awaiting my response. I'd been sitting here drinking for a while now; the vodka had loosened my lips, and I needed to vent. At this point I didn't care that

I didn't know this woman from Adam, so I continued with my monologue of despair.

"You know what? I worked at that firm for seven years, and I was a model employee. They should've fired Sanchez," I said, finishing my most recent shot of vodka and swaying on my bar stool. "Joey, can I get another shot over here, please?" If he heard me, he didn't respond. Damn it, I needed another drink.

Okay, so maybe I hadn't been a model employee, but I hadn't deserved to get fired. Sure, over the years I had liberated a few office supplies, been caught kissing the mailroom clerk in the copy room, and forgotten to bring chili on potluck days. So sue me. Pun intended. However, the results of yesterday's game between the Tennessee Titans and the Atlanta Falcons had left Sanchez in a mood. Everyone in the office knew to avoid Sanchez when the Falcons lost. Sanchez was a Tennessee transplant from Atlanta and a diehard Falcons fan. I should say everyone in the office knew this except me. Not being a sports fan myself, I didn't understand the pain one experiences when one's team loses. And boy, had they lost. Tennessee had handed them their asses.

"Aren't the Falcons the team that lost the Super Bowl 28-3 that time?" I said casually as I poured myself a cup of coffee while some coworkers talked about the game in the break room.

Complete silence filled the room. Everyone turned to stare at me in horror.

"What?" I asked, glancing down at my blouse, wondering if I'd missed a button while dressing this morning. Then I turned to look behind me, following the gazes of my coworkers. There stood Sanchez, seething. He fixed his murderous expression on me and if looks could kill, well, I would've been pushing up daisies already.

"What did you say, Jones?" Sanchez asked through gritted teeth. His knuckles had grown white, threatening to decimate the Styrofoam cup of coffee he held. He moved towards me and I instinctively took a step backwards, bumping into the vending machine at my back.

"I—uh, I mean, they lost the Super Bowl, right? Wasn't that them, the Falcons?" I said, still unaware of my error. I tried to collect myself, smoothing my skirt after my near collision with the Coke machine.

I heard a collective gasp. Avery, the intern, covered her mouth and looked at me with wide eyes. Mike, the mailroom clerk I'd kissed in the copy room that time, almost imperceptibly shook his head at me. Peggy from Accounting crossed herself and glanced away when I looked at her.

The Styrofoam cup in Sanchez's hand was threatening to buckle under his grasp and I could see a vein in his forehead throb. His black eyes were full of rage, and it was all directed at me now.

"In my office. Now, Jones!" he spat through gritted teeth. Sanchez tossed the cup into a nearby trash can on his way out of the break room, sending the remains of his coffee spattering everywhere.

"Did I say something wrong?" I asked, turning to look at my coworkers with bewilderment.

After I finished telling her of my horrible day, Farrah Fawcett, whose name I had gathered was Doreen Jenkins, commiserated with my story. Somehow, she'd snagged the bottle of vodka from behind the counter while Joey was busy with other patrons. Doreen mercifully filled my shot glass once again and passed it to me.

"That Sanchez sounds like a real ass," she said in a rather nasally, raspy voice, while inhaling more vapors. I laughed.

"Ass. Abernathy, Smith, and Sanchez. And they can kiss mine!"

"So, what happened next, hun? Did he fire you?" Doreen said, urging me on. It was getting late; the other patrons had been filing out the door in small groups here and there until finally Doreen and I were on our own. Joey had cleaned up the bar and was busy putting upside down chairs on top of tables so he could vacuum later. He glanced at us now and then with raised eyebrows, but I knew he probably didn't mind us lingering. I sighed.

"Well, when I arrived in Sanchez's office, he started yelling at me so loudly that he drew a crowd— which included the head of HR. She ended up pulling us both into her office. She reprimanded him for losing his shit so hard over a football game that he lost it all over again. But since he's a partner—the second S in ASS, remember?" I continued, "I was the one who got fired. She said it made for an unsafe work environment to have a subordinate provoking a partner into that kind of violent response." I rolled my eyes and downed the shot of vodka that remained in front of me and noticed that the bottle was now empty. Damn it.

"Oh sweetie, that's horrible. So unfair," Doreen said in a consoling tone as she continued to vape. I noticed her looking at her watch, which reminded me of how late it was. Mac, my fifteen-year-old daughter, was probably at home dressed in black pj's, having just finished a vegan frozen meal for dinner and was wondering why I wasn't home yet. Hopefully Grandma was at home on the other side of the duplex, keeping an eye on things. Or maybe she was down at Forever Young, the assisted living home where Gus lived. I really didn't want to think about that possibility though.

"I've gotta close up, ladies. Cricket, hang out here for a few minutes and I'll give you a ride home, okay? I just need to finish up a couple things," Joey said, having appeared beside me as he gently touched my shoulder.

I turned to answer him and was newly struck by his dark good looks. Joey was tall, dark, and handsome. It was easy to forget when I'd known him for so long and we had such an easy friendship between us. He cocked an eyebrow at me and ran a hand through his wavy brown hair. And those sparkling brown eyes… Oh man, I thought as a tingly feeling shot through me while meeting his gaze. I could get in a lot of trouble if I let him drive me home tonight, I thought. I've had too much to drink and I might take advantage of him, being all unintentionally sexy like he is.

I glanced at Doreen, my new BFF, who had made no move to leave even after hearing Joey say he was about to lock up.

"Joey, it's ok. I think Doreen here might give me a lift. I don't want to be a bother…" I trailed off, eyeing his muscular arms again. Am I crazy, I thought? I'm crazy, I confirmed. I'm also drunk, I reminded myself. I turned to Doreen to see how she had received the news that she was now driving me home. She looked pleased about it.

"Sure, sweetie, no problem." She beamed at me, taking another pull of Tutti Frutti and exhaling the sweet-smelling vapors in my general direction. She grabbed a large, hot pink satchel on the barstool next to her and stood up. It was then I noticed Doreen was indeed wearing jelly shoes. Sweet baby Jesus, I thought, trying not to laugh and failing.

Joey frowned at me, then at Doreen, then back at me.

"No offense—I'm sorry, what is your name?" he said, but didn't wait for a reply before continuing. "Cricket, you just met her. Wait around a couple minutes and I'll drop you off at your place. It's on my way," He untied the dirty apron he wore and glanced at Doreen again with disdain. "Be right back, don't move," he told me, then disappeared into the swinging double doors behind the bar.

"Come on babe, let's hit the road," Doreen said, taking my arm. I stood up and immediately noticed there were little fishies inside my head doing backflips. Woah, that's not supposed to happen. I sat back down.

"I'm supposed to wait," I said weakly, pulling my arm out of her grasp. Suddenly, I didn't feel well.

"Why wait, Shug? I can take you now. Come on," she insisted, a sense of urgency creeping into her raspy voice. Again, she took my elbow and urged me up from the barstool and grabbed my bag and looped it over my head. "There's something I want to talk to you about, anyway, and we need some privacy." Doreen steered me towards the front door and I didn't resist.

7

I glanced behind us as we walked, but Joey was still in the back. I'll just call him tomorrow... err, later today, and explain, I thought. I let her lead me out of the bar and onto the street where there was a black car already waiting by the entrance, with tinted windows. It looked expensive.

"Wait, is this your car?" I slurred. She opened the back-passenger side door and unceremoniously shoved me in. After a moment, the little fishies in my brain settled down again and Doreen opened the back door on the other side and climbed in beside me.

"Drive," she commanded, and a previously unnoticed figure behind the wheel complied. The car moved. It suddenly struck me that maybe this wasn't a good idea after all. Doreen turned her attention to me and beamed.

"Ok sweetie, now we can talk. I couldn't risk anyone overhearing this—I was so glad when you mentioned I should give you a ride home!" I blinked and tried to comprehend.

"Yeah, it was a brilliant idea... your car is nice," I said, my words running together. Why did my mouth have cotton balls in it? Doreen giggled.

"Wait, I didn't tell you my address," I said, squinting at her.

She ignored me and went on. "It's so lucky you lost your job today, I'm telling you, hun," she said as she began vaping again, considerately blowing the fumes away from me. "My boss is looking for someone just like you. When I saw you and heard your story, I knew you'd be perfect."

She smiled and pressed a business card into my hand. I looked down at it through bleary eyes. It appeared to be a regular-sized business card, black, with a phone number embossed on it. That was all. Just a number.

"What... who..." I began, desperately trying to hold on to my consciousness and the vodka I had consumed earlier. The driver wasn't helping matters either, taking curves and turns more quickly than my stomach would've liked. I swallowed hard as the contents of my stomach threatened to come up and the car lurched forward again.

"Just call the number tomorrow... I mean, later today," she giggled. I realized I was being driven home in a strange car with a middle-aged woman I'd only just met who looked like she walked off an 80s movie set. And that she'd given me a mysterious business card and told me to call the number tomorrow while she giggled. And then I started giggling. Uncontrollably.

"You'll be glad you did. I promise," she said, smiling sweetly at me. She patted my hand affectionately while the car came to a sudden halt. I glanced at the card again and then stuck it in my bra. Good a place as any, right? I grabbed my bag and before I could reach for the handle, the driver opened the door for me. We were in front of my duplex, and every light in the place was on. Great, I thought.

The driver held out a hand and helped me out of the car without a word. I noticed he was tall and wearing all black while I clumsily made my way out of the backseat. He held me steady while he walked me up the short driveway and then up the steps of my porch.

"Good luck, honey!" Doreen called.

My attendant rang the doorbell for me and left me to my own devices. I grabbed the porch railing to keep from falling over as I heard the car drive away. My stomach lurched just as the front door opened.

"Where the hell have you been, Mom?" Mac said.

I turned my head and vomited into the bushes.

Chapter 2

I awoke, after what I assumed was several hours of being passed out, in my bed. I was still wearing my work clothes. Thanks, Mac. She had at least removed my boots, and I thanked her silently for that. If memory served me, it was Saturday. Which meant that I didn't have to get up and go to work. Oh, wait. I don't have a job anymore, I remembered, groaning. I rolled over and immediately threw my arm over my eyes to block the hateful bright light streaming into my room. There weren't quite as many little fishies swimming in my head this morning, so that was a wonderful thing.

Coffee. I needed it. I rolled out of the bed and stood up with some effort. I took a few baby steps as yesterday came flooding back to me. Getting fired, getting drunk at The Rusty Nail, Joey, Doreen, the weird drive home. Vomiting on the porch. Oh, no. Grandma Betty would be pissed if I had gotten puke on her begonias. And Joey. I'd have to call him later to explain what happened. But first, coffee.

I stumbled from my bedroom, down the hall, through the living room, and into the kitchen. There was no sign of Mac. She was probably hanging out at Starbucks with a group of mopey, black clad teenagers who were lamenting the drudgery of their existence. I rolled my eyes. Ouch, that hurt. While I got a pot of coffee going, I heard some noise outside. I went to the window to investigate and sucked in my breath when the bright light hit my eyes.

Shielding them, I tried again and noticed a massive blond man wearing tight jeans, black boots, a black t-shirt, and a black leather vest. Black line work tattoos covered his muscular arms and his fingers held many silver rings. His short blond hair stood in haphazard spikes on top of his head and he sported a five o'clock shadow which indicated he hadn't shaved recently. Sexy, I thought, biting my lip and enjoying the view. Then I noticed he was standing by a black Harley-Davidson motorcycle in the driveway I shared with my Grandma's side of the duplex. That snapped me out of it. What the hell was a biker doing at Grandma's? Forgetting my need for coffee and that I was barefoot and sporting bed hair, I flung the door open and marched out on to the porch where the man was now bent over inspecting the flowers.

Hearing me approach, he looked up. Sparkling, deep blue eyes met mine, the corners crinkling in a smile. His jawline was that of a Greek God, enhanced by the slight stubble that was visible, and the tattoos I had noticed from inside the house were so much more impressive up close. This guy had muscles everywhere... and I mean Every. Where. I almost forgot that I should find out what he was doing in my yard. He rose to his feet, wiping dirt from his hands before extending one to me.

"Alright? Cricket, I assume?" he asked, still smiling. At the sound of his British accented, husky voice pronouncing my name, I nearly lost control of my legs. I reached out to grab his hand, not necessarily to shake it, but to help regain my balance. Get it together, Cricket, I mentally rebuked myself.

"Yes, and you are?" I croaked while doing a terrible job of not ogling him. For a moment I imagined what it might be like to kiss those pouty lips and wrap my arms around his muscular body, when I noticed the aforementioned lips smirking. I blinked and looked up at the enormous man, gaining control of myself once again.

"Well?" I asked, crossing my arms in front of me. I mentally shoved my inner ho out of the way. This is not the time, Ho Cricket.

"I'm Zeb, your new neighbor. Just noticing these begonias are in shambles." He gestured towards the vomit encrusted begonias near the porch with a frown. Oh yeah, I thought, suppressing a grimace. Wait, did he say *neighbor*?

"I'm sorry, you can't be my neighbor," I said, shielding my eyes from the sun as he turned away from the flowers and back to me. "My grandmother lives in the other side of this duplex and as you can tell, there's not much else around here," I said, nodding my head towards the road where the nearest neighboring house was just a speck on the horizon. "Unless you're planning to live under that rock over there, I think you're lost," I smiled charmingly at him and wished that I had brushed my hair before coming outside to interrogate him.

Hey, nothing wrong with flirting a little, especially now that I've figured out that he's just a lost, sexy, biker dude who somehow found himself on my doorstep in Bitter End, Tennessee. Lucky me, Ho Cricket thought.

Zeb looked like he was preparing to reply when the door to the opposite side of the duplex opened and Grandma Betty came tottering out.

"Cricket! I'm so glad you're up, I wanted to introduce you to Sebastian Walker, your new neighbor. I've leased my side of the duplex to him!" Grandma

13

beamed up at Zeb and patted his shoulder, lingering a little too long over his bicep. She patted her hair and simpered at him while I stared back and forth between the two of them in disbelief.

"Actually, I go by Zeb," he interjected, looking between the two of us. I kept my attention on Grandma.

"What do you mean, 'leased your side of the duplex'? Where are you planning to live?" I asked with a huff, crossing my arms and glaring at the two of them. *If she says she's moving in with Gus at Forever Young, I'm going to—*

"I'm moving in with Gus at Forever Young!" she said happily, cutting off my thoughts. She grinned at me, then at Zeb. Grandma was a plump little lady in her eighties, but she had more energy than me most of the time. She sported a silver bobbed hairdo, a pair of large rose gold-framed glasses, and a white crocheted handbag, which she was rarely parted from. Wearing a short, pink floral dress and white patent leather flats, she was ready to show those bitches at Forever Young who was in charge. Grandma Betty was always all sass and attitude, and today was no different.

I pinched the bridge of my nose, took a deep breath, and closed my eyes momentarily. My dearly departed mother's last words to me were, "Don't let your Grandma do anything stupid, Cricket," fully knowing how difficult that task would be. I heaved a sigh. *Moving in with her boyfriend of only a couple weeks probably qualified as stupid,* I thought with exasperation.

"Grandma, you've known Gus for what, two weeks? I don't think it's a good idea," I glanced at Zeb who stood to the side, hands on hips, and looked from

14

one of us to the other with a bewildered expression on his handsome face. God, where did she find him? I thought to myself. Has she been on Tinder again? I'd take that up with Grandma later. She frowned.

"I don't remember asking your permission. I am an independent woman, and I am old enough to make my own decisions. Now stop being rude in front of Zeb. Zeb, this is my granddaughter, Cricket. Remember, I told you about her? She's not usually like this. From what I gather, she had a rough night and came home rather late," Grandma narrowed her eyes at me. "And I know what happened to the begonias, young lady," she added. Zeb's eyebrows shot up as he looked from me to the flowers. Thanks a lot, Grandma.

"Okay, let's discuss this. Zeb, it was nice to meet you. I'm sorry she's wasted your time; I think you should start looking for someplace else to rent," I took Grandma's arm and steered her towards my door. That didn't go over so well. She jerked her arm away from me and rooted herself in place on the walkway.

"Cricket, don't treat me like I'm a child. I thought you'd be more supportive of my relationship with Gus, and frankly, I'm disappointed in how you're acting," she said, glaring at me. "Zeb, would you mind helping me bring my bags to the car?" She sent one last glance my way and then turned to Zeb with a smile. He seemed at a loss for what to do, a look of bewilderment on his face as he met Grandma's gaze. I threw my hands up in the air in exasperation.

"Fine, go. Don't come crying to me in a week when things aren't working out with Gus and you're ready to move back in. Oh wait, you won't be able to because you've just leased out your side of the duplex."

I scowled at them both before marching back to my side of the porch. I went inside the house and slammed the door behind me.

"Gah!" I yelled to the empty room. The coffee was ready. The aroma filled the air and made my mouth water. "Right, coffee. NOW," I said out loud to myself as I grabbed a mug and poured some sweet-smelling brew into it. Just then, my cell phone started blaring "Sweet Child of Mine" by Guns N Roses. I picked it up and looked at the screen... The Rusty Nail. Great, now I'd have to explain myself to Joey, I thought and groaned.

"Hello?" I answered, after taking a sip from my mug and closing my eyes in bliss as the coffee hit my tongue.

"What the hell happened to you last night, Cricket?" Joey said without bothering to say hello. His slight southern accent was more pronounced when he was angry, I noted. I sat down on the couch, cradling my steaming mug of coffee, phone tucked between my ear and my shoulder, and waited for him to continue.

"As soon as I realized you had left, I jumped in my truck and drove to your place. I saw you being helped to your door by some guy while that lady you were talking to waited in the car. And then I saw Mac letting you in, so I knew you were alright. But damn, girl. That was a shitty thing you did to leave after I asked you to wait. You were so drunk, anything could've happened," Joey said, ending with an exasperated sigh. I could hear the anger in his voice fizzling out by the time he stopped talking though.

"Joey, I'm sorry. I wasn't feeling well, and Doreen said she could take me straight home so I

16

wouldn't have to wait for you. It seemed like a good idea at the time. Forgive me?" I really poured the charm on thick for that last part. I thought Joey had a low-key crush on me, so I figured I had an advantage here. He sighed heavily on the other end of the line.

"Yes, I forgive you. Shit. Come to the bar later, okay?" I agreed that I would and ended the call. I glanced back outside and Grandma and Zeb were gone; I assumed he had helped her load her bags into her car and she was headed to Forever Young by now. Who knows where he went, but his bike was gone. How am I going to fix this? She can't move in with Gus, I thought, as I continued to sip my coffee and tried to think of a solution.

I leaned back in my recliner, ready to let the coffee work its magic on my hangover when I felt something scratch my left boob. What the—I frowned and reached into my bra, pulling out a black business card with a phone number embossed on it. Oh, yeah. Doreen gave it to me last night and told me to call it today. Something about her boss needed to hire someone, and she thought I'd be perfect for the job? I sighed. Well, I am unemployed now and I have a teenager to feed, clothe, and send to MIT in a few more years, not to mention all the other bills that would keep rolling in regardless of my job situation. Including the debt my ex-husband had accumulated in my name with his half-baked business ideas. I sighed again.

Maybe I should call the number and just find out what the job is, I thought. If it was stripping, I'm out. I made a promise to my mother once that I'd stay off the pole and I would not go back on that now, no matter how dire the circumstances. As I flipped the card back and forth between my fingers and thought about it, Mac came tumbling in through the door, clad in all black, as was customary these days. She slung her long, black hair behind her shoulder and flung her huge backpack onto the couch.

"God, Mom, I can't believe you," she said, in that teenage, self-righteous tone of voice she'd gotten so good at lately. She stood in front of me with her arms crossed. I groaned and put the business card back into my bra. "So, when I get drunk and stay out all night, I don't want to hear anything about it," she continued.

"Excuse me, you are underage. There will be no getting drunk and staying out all night for you for many years to come," I said. "Besides, I had an excuse. I got fired yesterday. But it'll be okay, I already have a lead on another job." I sat my coffee cup on the table next to me and rubbed my temples. Mac glared at me.

Mackenzie Grace, my fifteen-year-old daughter, was a beauty. She had my long blonde hair, which she had recently dyed jet black, to my utter disappointment. She had her dad's green eyes and was tall, willowy, and slender. And she had a sarcastic mouth on her that wouldn't quit. I wonder where she got that from?

"Whatever. I'm going over to Luther's house to study. Unless you need me to hold your hair back while you vomit on Grandma's flowers again," Mac said over her shoulder, as she headed for the kitchen.

"Har har," I said, raising my voice slightly so she could still hear me. "What are you and Luther studying? Will his parents be home?" I said, trying to change the subject from my escapades of last night. I held my head as it throbbed. She returned to the living room with a cold bottle of water and rolled her black lined, perfectly smoked eyes at me.

"Yeah, his parents will be there. We have a project due for Chemistry class that we're going to work on." She grabbed her backpack and made for the door without waiting for a response.

"Wait, what about dinner?" I called just before she closed the door behind her. I promise, I am an excellent mom most of the time when I'm not getting fired, drunk, accepting rides from strangers, and vomiting in the bushes. She sighed.

"His mom is cooking dinner. You should try doing that sometime," Mac smiled sweetly and shut the door behind her as she left. What did I do to deserve the punishment of having a daughter just like me, I wondered.

I puttered around the house for a while, doing the standard weekend chores while blasting classic rock through the speakers. I also tried to rectify the situation with the begonias, but I was thinking they were a lost cause. It was several hours before I remembered the business card again. I pulled it out of my bra and stared at it. Seriously, I have to stop sticking stuff in there. After examining it for a minute, I thought, what the hell? I picked up my cell phone and dialed the number. It didn't even ring before a squeaky female voice answered in a thick southern drawl.

"Hello, thank you for calling Sunshine Cleaners! How may I help you?"

I pulled the phone away from my ear and looked at it. I looked at the card. Yep, I dialed the right number. I replaced the phone to my ear. I'm unemployed, I don't have many options, I reminded myself.

"Hi. Okay, this will sound weird, but I met a lady named Doreen last night, and she gave me your card. She said that you may have a position available?" There was a giggle on the other end.

"Yes, Doreen told me to expect your call. I'm so sorry to hear that you lost your job." Her tone turned solemn at that last bit to demonstrate how very sorry she was. I had to appreciate the effort.

"Thanks. So what positions do y'all have available? Doreen didn't tell me anything about it. You're a dry cleaner?" I began. God, I'm gonna have to work at a dry cleaner. I'd heard horror stories about chemicals and injuries before from a friend whose family had owned one. Whatever pays the bills, Cricket, I reminded myself.

"You'll have to speak to Carl," the squeaky, southern voice replied. "Actually, he will want to meet with you to explain. Can you come by in a few hours, maybe around 9 p.m.?" Interesting. A top-secret position at the dry cleaner. Maybe they launder money. Maybe I should just hang up, I thought. Just then, Squeaky, as I'd begun calling my nameless contact at Sunshine Cleaners, spoke up.

"I don't know what positions are available, but I can tell you one thing though, the pay is excellent." Now we were getting somewhere.

"Sure, I can come by tonight… but why so late?" I said, grabbing a pen and paper from the coffee table to take down the address. Squeaky just giggled as she told me the address in downtown Nashville. What the hell was I getting myself into?

Chapter 3

I pulled my old minivan into the parking lot of Sunshine Cleaners in a seedy part of downtown Nashville. This was it, no doubt about it. There was a gigantic sign out front with a cheesy cartoon sun smiling at a basket of laundry, lit up by a spotlight which made it visible in the black sky. Charming, I thought, and rolled my eyes. I sighed and checked my makeup in the rear-view mirror. My cheeks were rosy enough, blue eyes perfectly lined, and I'd even applied some fake eyelashes which I'd started using recently after Mac had showed me how to apply them. I dabbed on more of the "Unicorn Blood" red lipstick, also courtesy of Mac, and smiled into the mirror to make sure I didn't have any on my teeth. I wore my long blonde hair loose and spilling over one shoulder.

I wore one of my best paralegal outfits from my previous job. Black pencil skirt, white button up blouse tucked in, a close-fitting black blazer, and black heels. Now that I was here though, I felt a little overdressed. I didn't think the happy sunshine on the logo cared about my expensive blazer.

"What am I doing?" I said aloud. This is ridiculous. I should just start the van, go home and look at the want ads while drowning my sorrows in a couple of bottles of wine like a normal person. As I was about to leave to do just that I spotted Doreen coming out of the building, heading my way, smiling and waving. How did she know I was here? Sighing in defeat, I grabbed my purse and opened the door of the van.

"Sweetie! Vanessa told me you called, so I thought I'd meet you here. I'm so glad you're meeting

21

Carl!" Doreen tottered towards me as I met her halfway in the dark, almost empty parking lot. Once again, she was sporting 1980s fashion. This time, it was a bright yellow micro mini skirt paired with an off the shoulder oversized pink top. Her poufy hair was in a side pony, complete with animal print scrunchie. She wore hot pink lipstick, green eyeshadow, and large gold hoop earrings. Wow, I thought. I mean, that's really all there was to say.

I smiled weakly at her. "Hey Doreen, long time no see," I said, to which she giggled.

She grabbed my arm and steered me towards the front door of Sunshine Cleaners. Vanessa, formerly known as Squeaky, sat at a large curved desk right inside the door. She had short brown hair, black-framed glasses, and wore a plaid skirt with a cute green cardigan. She wore a headset and was busy writing on a nearby notepad while squeaking "uh huh" repeatedly to whoever was on the other end of the line. She glanced up at us and waved, shooting us a bright smile and indicated that we should have a seat on the couch across from her.

I looked around as I sat down. It seemed the entire building was leftover from circa 1975, not just the sign outside. Gold and orange reigned in the color scheme, and the carpet was a brown shag. I was growing more confused and concerned by the minute. What could they possibly hire me to do here? I know nothing about dry cleaning. And how could they afford to pay me "excellently" as Vanessa had promised if they couldn't even bring their property into the 21st century? Doreen sat beside me on the gold couch and I

leaned over and whispered, "I'm not sure about this…"
I trailed off.

Doreen smiled again, reassuringly. "Oh honey,
just wait until you meet Carl. He'll love you! And
you're gonna love working here, I can promise you
that," she continued in her sweet southern drawl while
firing up her vaping device. Today's flavor was Gummi
Bear. We sat silently, listening to a blend of 1970s
elevator music being piped softly out of the overhead
speakers while Vanessa continued her banter of "uh
huh" and "right" over the headset.

A few minutes crept by and I felt more and
more like this was all a massive, gargantuan,
humongous, awful idea. I started feeling a weird tingly
sensation in my chest, which I concluded meant either I
was having a heart attack or that I should get the hell
out of here. I was this close to grabbing my bag and
making a run for the door when the side door opened
and out stepped who I could only assume was Carl.

He was of average height, light brown hair that
swept over his eyes in the front giving him a boyish
look. Probably in his early thirties, very fair skinned,
and his eyes were a striking shade of brown mixed with
gold. Whiskey-colored, I would call it. He looked
professional in a navy blue suit, white shirt, and blue
and brown striped tie, which he wore loose around his
neck. His eyes swept over us, and he motioned for us to
follow him. He didn't smile. Doreen and I were
gathering our bags when he said, "Just her." I looked at
Doreen, and she shrugged.

"I'll wait for you here, sweetie," she said,
patting my arm and sitting back down to continue her
vaping.

Hesitantly, I rose and followed Carl into his office, which was much more modern than the parts of the building that I had seen so far. Everything was white and sterile looking. His desk was a glossy white, the carpet was white, the filing cabinets were white. I guess he takes cleanliness seriously, I thought, remembering this was in fact a dry cleaning business. Or was it? I thought. He indicated that I should have a seat in one of the white chairs across from his desk. He sat in the large white captain's chair behind the desk and looked at me. And continued to look at me in silence for what seemed to stretch into several minutes. I bit my lip. I glanced at the wall, then I met his eyes again.

"So," I said, trailing off. If this wasn't awkward, I didn't know what was.

"Doreen has told us about you. You were a skilled paralegal at a Nashville law firm and recently lost your job. You have a teenage daughter, your parents are deceased, your grandmother lives next door to you. You're divorced, not seeing anyone, and have an unnatural affinity for coffee and wine. Anything else we should know?" Carl spoke matter-of-factly in an accent that sounded vaguely Russian. He placed his hands together under his chin and waited for my response.

"I guess not. Except my grandmother just moved out," I said weakly. I pulled my already tight blazer closer around myself. How did he know all that stuff? And who said my love of coffee was unnatural? This had to be the weirdest job interview in the history of job interviews.

"Alright, then. Now I need to tell you what the job entails. If I tell you, that means you have agreed to work for us and that you will never divulge our secrets to anyone. Ever. The penalty is more than you would want to pay, I assure you," he spoke quickly and softly, eyes focused on mine.

"Wait. So, before you'll tell me what the job is, I'll have to accept the job... without knowing what the job is? That doesn't make sense," I started. What the hell kind of game was he playing here? I made a move to stand up, and he put one hand up in a stop motion.

Just then, another door opened, and a young lady entered the room. She was also pale skinned like Carl. She wore her beautiful red hair pulled back into a slick ponytail and she wore a plain black shift dress. Her eyes were the same whiskey color as Carl's and her lips were very red against her fair skin. Even redder than the "Unicorn Blood" lipstick I was wearing. Was this his sister? Maybe Sunshine Cleaners was a family business? This just keeps getting weirder, I thought, and I wished that I had told Joey or Grandma or someone that I was coming here tonight. No one will ever know what became of me, I thought wearily. Who will keep Mac in vegan snacks and black clothing after I'm gone?

"Ms. Jones, I believe you will happily accept the job once you learn how much we will pay for your discretion. You will never have to wonder how you will send your daughter to MIT again. You'll be able to buy the law firm of Abernathy, Smith, and Sanchez and fire them all if you so desire."

He rose from his desk and turned to the young lady who had seated herself on a stool in the middle of the room. "Alexandra, darling. Please show Ms. Jones."

He walked to her side and gently laid a hand on the girl, Alexandra's, arm. She smiled warmly up at him, then turned her gaze to me. As I smiled back at her, two sharp pointy fangs slowly let down from either side of her upper row of teeth.

"What the—" I began. My smile faded as the fangs continued to grow from Alexandra's grin. I looked at Carl, then back to Alexandra, then at the door.

"My dear, what you see here in front of you is a vampire. Despite what the human world wants you to believe, we are real. We exist among you and always have. Some humans in specific positions of power have known about us over the years and have made treaties and various agreements with us in the past, but this knowledge is on a need to know basis only." He strode back to his desk and sat down, folding his hands beneath his chin as he held my disbelieving gaze.

"Why am I telling you this? Because we need humans we can trust who can carry out our business for us when we are—indisposed—during certain hours. We pay our people well for their honesty, their loyalty, and their discretion on our behalf. You will be what we call a Daytime Concierge for one of our highest officials in the Nashville Ministry of Vampire Affairs. She recently… lost her former attendant." Carl finally stopped talking while I gawked at Alexandra's fangs and then at Carl, listening but not believing what I was hearing.

I sat silently for a minute and then began laughing. Carl and Alexandra exchanged puzzled looks while I continued to giggle uncontrollably. "Wait, wait, wait…" I said, trying to stifle my snickering. "Who put you up to this? Seriously, very believable. I'm impressed. The fangs look super real. But I'm trying to find an actual job so if you don't mind, I'm going now. Thanks for the laugh though, really." I collected my bag and rose from my seat, still catching my breath from laughing so hard. Carl appeared in front of me, blocking my way. How did he move so quickly? I thought.

"Ms. Jones, I do not joke. You need a job and we need someone like you." He pulled an index card from his inside jacket pocket and an envelope and handed them to me. "This is your starting salary and your signing bonus. Do we have an agreement?"

I smirked at him and took the card. My eyes nearly popped out of my head when I saw all the zeros. My mouth hung wide open. I looked up to see Carl's satisfied smile. Then I tore the envelope open and had a minor stroke when I saw the check.

Cricket, you can work for crazy people who think they are vampires for a while, right? For this much money? I asked myself. My God, the signing bonus alone would solve so many financial problems. So what if Carl and Alexandra were bat shit crazy? I had worked with crazy people before at ASS, right? And I didn't have any other options on the table at this point. So, I might have to go grocery shopping for some old lady who sleeps all day because she's convinced she'll go up in flames if she ventures out into in the daylight. I can handle that, at least for now.

I cleared my throat while shoving the index card and envelope into my purse. "Carl, we have an agreement. When do I start?"

Chapter 4

After the meeting with Carl, I took a few moments alone in the bathroom to review the index card and contents of the envelope. I couldn't get over how much money they were offering me. I was still reeling and in disbelief of the story they had told me, so I tried to collect myself as best I could before rejoining Doreen, who was still waiting for me in the lobby. Once I did, she insisted on taking me to The Rusty Nail to celebrate my new job. She also wanted to give me the lowdown on what to expect in my new position. Since I knew next to nothing about what being a Daytime Concierge for the Ministry of Vampire Affairs entailed, I agreed.

We sat in a booth and I listened to her talk about Carl, Alexandra, and other vampires I hadn't met yet as I admired Joey from afar while he worked the bar. He caught me looking at him and winked. I smiled back and turned my attention to what Doreen was saying.

"So, honey, the vampires sleep from dawn until dusk. Some of the older ones can stay up later and wake up earlier, but those are few and far between. Like Nina, she's the one you'll be working for, she's pretty old so she may be able to do it." Doreen took out her vaping device as she spoke. Stoned Smurf was the flavor of the day.

I'd been told that Nina Lambert, the vampire who I would assist, was the Director of the Nashville branch of the Ministry of Vampire Affairs. That was the equivalent of the Governor of Tennessee, from what I gathered. I was still having some trouble believing this stuff was real. I was expecting Allen Funt to jump out from behind a potted plant and yell, "Surprise! You're on Candid Camera!"

"What about drinking blood? Is she gonna suck my blood? I'm not ok with that," I said, taking a pull from the beer I was nursing. If this was for real, I was getting a little nervous. I mean, I've never worked for an alpha predator before. If Nina decided she wanted my blood, how would I possibly be able to protect myself? Maybe I should read the contract Carl had given me to find out if blood donation was part of the job description.

Doreen giggled. "Shug, you probably won't even see her. She'll leave you notes. She'll text you and email you instructions. And even if you ever do see her, Nina is old. I mean, centuries old. She has herself under control. I mean, she has to, right? She's the Director of the MVA," she concluded. Sounded logical. "Besides, they have that synthetic blood now so they rarely do live feedings from humans. Most of them drink synthetic. There's B+, Sanguine O, and Perfect Plasma, among others," she continued. "They even make dessert and alcoholic blood!" Doreen said, exhaling clouds of vapor while she spoke.

"Good to know I'm not the only thing on the menu," I said wearily. "What else should I know about these *vampires*? Honestly, Doreen, I'm having a little trouble believing this is not bullshit," I continued, taking a pull from my lukewarm beer. I still believed this was some elaborate hoax. How could vampires be real?

She giggled. "Well, they're definitely real. And they can move super fast. Some of them have other powers like flying, but it's rare. Let's see, what else…"

Doreen stopped to take a sip of her beer while she thought. "Oh yeah, silver burns them so if you have any silver jewelry, don't wear it around Nina. The garlic thing is false, though. Oh, and they can see their reflections in mirrors too," she concluded as I spotted Joey approaching.

He smiled at me and placed a couple of cold beers on the table. He was looking hot, as usual, and I felt a spark of electricity run through me at the sight of him. What was wrong with me? How long had I known Joey and only now was I starting to look at him and wonder what it would be like to run my hands through that thick, wavy hair of his and guide his mouth slowly to mine and—

"Cricket? You ok, doll?" Joey said, frowning slightly at my obvious space out moment. "Maybe you don't need another one of these." He winked as he passed a cold beer to me and took the half empty bottle from my hand.

I smiled and took a drink. Yeah, something was definitely wrong with me called "I've been celibate since my divorce 18 months ago". But that was a problem to address at another time and most likely, not with Joey. He was my friend, I had to stop it. Go away, Ho Cricket, I rebuked my alter ego.

"Guess what? Cricket got a new job! Isn't that great!" Doreen said to Joey, beaming like a proud parent. His gaze shifted to me, curious and concerned.

"I know, I'm as shocked as you are," I said, taking a drink of the beer. Doreen laughed. Suddenly, she jumped up from her seat and began waving in the general direction of a group of women who had just entered the bar.

"That's Suzy, I'll be right back, babe," she said as she tottered off to greet whichever one Suzy was. That left me alone with Joey.

He sat down in Doreen's vacated spot and looked at me with serious eyes. Seriously sexy eyes. "So, you found a job already? That was fast. Another law firm?" His voice was low and deep, etched with concern. I saw him glance in Doreen's direction.

"No, not another law firm. I got a job at Sunshine Cleaners. It's kind of a clerical position," I said, not meeting his eyes. Better get used to it, I told myself. I'll be lying to everyone I know about what kind of work I'm doing. Because "I'm a personal assistant for bat shit crazy people who think they're vampires" would not go over well. Not to mention the fact that Carl would probably have me drawn and quartered for spilling the beans.

"Sunshine Cleaners? That shitty dry cleaner over on 4th? Really?" He eyed me warily and sighed. "Look, I know you've been hanging out with Doreen lately but I'm not so sure she's someone you want to get mixed up with. I've seen her around, she's always with different men who seem to be involved in some shady business. Maybe it's the mob or something, I don't know. But I don't want you getting hurt, okay? I mean it," he said, placing his hand over mine and squeezing. Oh boy. The mafia. If he only knew, I giggled internally.

I gathered my wits and smiled at him. "It's sweet of you to worry, Joe, but it's fine. Really. It's just a boring desk job. Answering phones, opening mail, running errands, that sort of thing. I know it's not in the best area of town, but I'm a big girl. I can take care of myself." I nudged his elbow with the still half full beer bottle. I glanced in Doreen's direction and saw her deeply involved in an animated conversation with Suzy. "Hey, would you let Doreen know I'm heading home? It's been a long day and I'm beat. Plus, I need to rest up this weekend, I start work on Monday," I said, standing up and putting my bag on my shoulder.

"Sure, I can do that. Promise me you'll be careful though, okay?" He rose from where he had been sitting and cleared the bottles from the table, stopping to wait for my reply.

"Careful is my middle name," I said with a wink. He rolled his eyes as I turned to leave.

When I pulled the minivan into the driveway, I saw the now familiar black Harley-Davidson motorcycle parked in the opposite driveway. Zeb was outside, wearing jeans and a white t-shirt, which revealed even more of his tattoos. He had a full sleeve on his right arm, and it was beautiful. I could see branches, leaves, a full moon, and what looked like a grim reaper's scythe, among other illustrations. All black line work. Impressive, I thought. His blond hair shone in the moonlight and I noticed the stubble on his chin had turned into a proper beard. I had to admit; he was hot. Was he tending to the flowers in Grandma Betty's yard? What was it with him and plants, I wondered.

I hadn't spoken to Grandma since she'd left in a huff the day before, and that worried me. I couldn't let her lease her side of the duplex out and live with Gus, who she barely knew. Thanks to my promise to my dearly departed mother, I had to watch out for Grandma. So, I figured now was as good a time as any to talk to Zeb about the situation. I turned the van off, got out and strode over to where he was watering the previously vomited upon begonias.

"Alright, Cricket?" he said as I approached, turning that stunning smile on me. It disarmed me briefly, but I decided I had to fix this situation Grandma had thrown us into, regardless of how sexy he was.

Zeb couldn't stay here, I had to get Grandma to move out of Gus's place and come back home. So yeah, unfortunately, Zeb couldn't stay, I thought to myself, once again admiring his well-muscled arms. Right. Here goes.

"Hey Zeb, so we probably need to talk about the whole Grandma Betty situation. Got a minute?" I said, keeping my cool. This would be harder than I thought. He's so nice and good-looking. I could let Grandma stay with Gus for a couple weeks, right? No, Cricket, you cannot, I scolded myself internally. You're right, Common Sense Cricket, I thought.

Zeb rose from the flower bed and said, "Sure, want to have a seat?" He gestured to the bright yellow double rocker glider on Grandma's porch. I followed him up the steps and sat down beside him while I tried to ignore the shiver that went down my spine as I did.

He turned to me and up close I could see how blue his eyes were. How pouty his lips were. How chiseled his jawline was. Boy, this would definitely be difficult.

"So, what's on your mind?" he said in that British accent that made my knees go weak, even though I was sitting down. It was like having Mr. Darcy sitting next to me.

"Look, I know that Grandma agreed to lease her side of the duplex to you, but honestly, this idea she has of moving in with Gus at Forever Young is ridiculous. She's only known him a couple weeks and she'll be ready to move back in here in another week or two, I'm sure of it. I guess what I'm asking is for you to please tell Grandma that you've changed your mind and find someplace else to live."

I finished and bit my lip as I met his eyes and waited for his response. Instead of being angry though, he looked amused. His mouth twitched as if he were trying to keep from laughing.

After a moment's pause, he said, "No."

No? That was it? Had I heard him correctly?

"What do you mean, 'no'?" I asked, irritably. I had asked nicely, and I had explained the situation. Hell, he was there when Grandma and I had butted heads over it the first time. And all he has to say about it is "no"?

"I mean no. Your Nan is a grown woman, Cricket. It's her property to do with as she likes and it's her business if she wants to shack up with some geezer she's known for half a day. We've signed a contract and I intend to stay." Zeb's eyes pierced mine as he spoke and there was still that hint of amusement on his stupid pouty lips.

"There are other places, even closer to Nashville, that you could rent. Why Bitter End? I'm asking nicely. Pretty please?" I said, putting all the sweetness I could muster behind those last words even though it irritated the hell out of me. "I can even help you find a place. I have connections," I said, forcing a smile.

"I appreciate the fact that you're looking out for your Nan, I really do. But this place is the perfect location for me and the job I've come here to do. I can't leave, not even if I wanted to," he said. Zeb's demeanor seemed to change with those last words. A seriousness washed over his face, and he glanced away from me.

"What job *did* you come here to do, by the way? I know nothing about you besides the fact that you're a mysterious, hot biker. If you insist on staying, you could at least tell me more about yourself. Like what you do for a living, where you came from, how long you intend to stay…" I trailed off, irritably. I noticed he was staring at me with a smirk on his annoying face.

"Well?" I continued, crossing my arms and glaring at him.

"You think I'm hot and mysterious, eh?" Zeb said, his eyes sparkling with amusement.

Crap, had I said that part out loud? I mentally slapped my forehead.

Answering none of my questions, he stood and said, "Well, I'll be seeing you around here, I expect. Good night, Cricket." He shot me a smile as he went inside, leaving me alone on the porch to stew.

I sighed and slumped back onto the rocker glider. Well, that hadn't gone as planned. I'll go to Forever Young and have a talk with Grandma tomorrow then, I thought. I determined I'd make her come home one way or another and if Zeb wouldn't help me, I'd have to figure something else out.

Just then a car came slowly up our driveway and stopped briefly, letting Mac out. She waved goodbye to the driver, who I assumed was Luther, and hauled her huge black backpack up the porch steps. She stopped when she caught sight of me, sitting on Grandma's side of the porch on the glider.

"What's up with you?" she said, dropping her backpack next to the door. "Waiting for the hot biker dude to come out and notice you?" she said as she came over to sit by me.

I playfully smacked her arm, "No, I'm trying to figure out a way to get Grandma to come home. I tried asking the hot biker dude to back out of the lease, but he said no." I sighed and laid my head on Mac's shoulder. She smelled like incense and sadness, and I figured that would please her if she knew. "Do you have any ideas?" I asked, picking up a lock of her long black hair and twirling it between my fingers.

She was quiet for a few beats before saying, "I don't know, maybe we could just let her do what she wants." I groaned. Why does everyone keep saying that?

Some strands of Mac's long black hair tickled my nose, so I raised my head and said, "Sorry I asked. Come inside. Have you eaten yet? I can make you a snack." I rose and headed for our door, and I heard her snort behind me at that.

"Thanks, but I'm not in the mood for a ketchup and potato chip sandwich, Mom," Mac said, grabbing her backpack and following me inside.

"Hey, you said you liked it," I said, closing the door behind us.

"I was five," Mac shot back at me, putting her earbuds in and heading up the stairs to her room.

I sighed, heading to the kitchen pantry to find myself a snack. It irritated me to discover that I was still thinking about Zeb and his annoyingly sexy lips as I dug a bag of chips out from behind a box of crackers. I frowned as I shoved a potato chip into my mouth, thinking. The man was maddening. How could I convince him to leave and get Grandma to move back home?

Chapter 5

The next day I headed over to Forever Young to pay Grandma and Gus a visit. It was on the outskirts of Metro Nashville, not too far from the duplex. I pulled the minivan into the parking lot, grabbed my bag, and headed in. There were elderly people in various states of activity everywhere. Some men were playing cards in the lobby while some ladies were crocheting in the corner near the fireplace. No sign of Grandma, though.

"Well hello there, doll face!" A man who looked to be well into his eighties shouted to me as I crossed the lobby to the reception desk. He was in a robe and his hair stuck up in every direction, but I figured that a compliment was a compliment, so I waved in his general direction as I approached the girl sitting at the desk.

"Excuse me, I'm looking for a man named Gus. I don't know his last name though, can you help?" The girl, who looked to be about eighteen, glanced up from her cell phone and rolled her eyes at me as she chewed her gum. She wore a Hello Kitty t-shirt and had pink streaks in her blonde hair.

"Lady, do you know how many old men named Gus we have here?" she said. Then, to illustrate her point, she raised her voice and said, "Hey, Gus!" I turned around and six different men were looking in our direction and another one was being tapped on the shoulder by a friend to let him know we had called for him. Great.

"Thanks for your help," I said with a sigh, moving away from the desk. I figured I'd have to roam the halls, listening for Grandma's shrill voice.

Thankfully, I didn't have to go very far before I heard her talking to someone.

"She forbade me to move in with Gus! Can you believe it, my own granddaughter, treating me like that!" The nurse that Grandma was speaking to just shook her head, so I marched over to interrupt.

"Speak of the devil huh, Grandma? Nice that you're telling all your new friends about me. Can we talk?" The nurse looked at me in disgust and moved away while Grandma huffed.

"Not if you're still not going to acknowledge my right to do what I want!" She crossed her arms and turned away from me, ironically looking like the child she claimed she wasn't.

I gently put a hand on her shoulder and turned her to face me. She was wearing a purple knee length dress with white slip-on shoes. She smelled like lavender and Bengay. She faced me but still refused to look at me. "Grandma, come on, we need to talk. I can't stand it when you're mad at me. Please?" I stuck my lower lip out and pouted at her. I could see her resolve melting.

"Okay, we can talk but I am not leaving here, Cricket. I've made up my mind!" She clutched her white crocheted purse and led me to two chairs near the ladies who were crocheting.

We sat, and I figured since she'd made it clear she wouldn't return home today, I'd move on to one of the other reasons I had visited her.

"Grandma, how did you meet Zeb? What do you know about him? Since you've abandoned Mac and I there with him living right next door, I think I deserve

40

to know more about him," I said. Yes, I played the guilt card right out of the gate. I'm shameless.

"He's such a nice boy, don't you think? Now that I think about it, you should date him, Cricket!" she said, beaming at the thought.

"Grandma, please," I said with a groan.

"We'll worry about setting that up later," she continued, ignoring me. "Let's see, I placed an ad on the Craigslist about renting my place out and he responded. We met for coffee and I told him all about the duplex, you, Mac, and of course, my plans to move in with my Gus. He paid for two months rent up front and signed a lease on the spot!" she said, clearly pleased with how it all went.

"What kind of work does he do? He mentioned needing to stay in our duplex to be close to his work, but he never told me what it was," I said.

And I was genuinely curious. What on earth could he do for a living that required him to live out in the country in a little area outside of Nashville known as Bitter End, in a duplex furnished with doilies and furniture covered in plastic? Was he involved in something illegal?

Maybe if I could find out what he was up to, Grandma would tear up her lease with him and move back home to protect Mac and I from the mean biker man. The chances of him being involved in illegal activities were probably slim, but I still wanted to know more about him. For research purposes, nothing more.

Grandma pursed her lips and thought for a moment. "You know, I don't think he ever told me either. We talked about everything else though!" She giggled. Good grief, my eighty-two-year-old grandma, smitten with Zeb. Yikes.

"Well, what did he tell you about himself? Or were you too busy admiring his muscles to pay attention?" I asked, irritably. She frowned at me.

"I was not! I would never, Cricket!" she protested. Yeah, yeah. So, it was becoming apparent to me that Grandma, being thoroughly charmed by the mysterious biker, didn't bother to find out squat about the man she leased her duplex to and allow to live next door to her two granddaughters. Thanks, Grandma.

I decided to move on to the last item on my list for today. "So, where's Gus? I'm dying to meet him," I said, glancing around the rec room as if I'd recognize him.

Grandma's eyes lit up at the mention of her beloved Gus. I mentally rolled my eyes. "Oh, he's busy with his work right now. I'd love for you to meet him, but he doesn't like me to disturb him while he's working. It takes him out of his zone, you know," she explained as if she knew all about Gus's zone.

"What kind of work could an eighty-two-year-old man who lives in a retirement community possibly do?" I wondered aloud. Grandma scowled and huffed.

"He works remotely, Cricket. That's the trend these days," she said with an exasperated sigh. She clearly didn't know what kind of work he was doing, and I was getting nowhere with my interrogation.

"*Dinner will be served in five minutes. Please make your way to the cafeteria, thank you,*" a sweet southern voice drawled over the intercom. Little old people began tottering in the cafeteria's direction, so I figured I might as well go. Since I didn't get to meet

Gus, that just meant I'd have to come back in a few days, I thought.

I stood and put my bag on my shoulder. "Well, you've been an enormous help, Detective Grandma. Thanks for thoroughly vetting your new tenant, my mind is now at ease."

She rolled her eyes at me and then smiled. "Cricket, thank you for coming down here. I know you love me in your own strange sort of way and that's why you try to run my life for me. But please stop, sweetie." She patted my cheek, and I resisted making a snarky comment.

"Besides, now that there's a hunky guy living next door to you, maybe you'll finally have a little fun of your own!" She giggled and tottered off before I could retort. Next time old lady, I thought. I sighed and headed for the exit.

Chapter 6

I awoke early on Monday morning in anticipation of an exciting first day of my new job. I had dressed in one of my best former paralegal ensembles—a pair of black skinny pants, a black button up blouse, a tan blazer, and leopard print pumps. I topped it off with a large black tote and a black beret. I felt very chic and ready to face a day of grueling orientation with the vampires.

I still had trouble saying *vampires* with a straight face. I wondered what I would learn today. Maybe I'd find out if they can turn into bats or if holy water would burn them. Basic Vampire 101 stuff.

I was just putting the finishing touches on my makeup and was about to grab my coffee and head out the door when my phone started buzzing and the sound of crickets chirping alerted me to an incoming text. I rolled my eyes and mentally made a note to make Mac change it back after school today. She wasn't even awake yet, preferring to allow herself about twenty minutes to get ready in time for Luther to pick her up for school.

I picked up the phone and read, "*Cricket. It's Nina. Please come to 1451 Lynnwood Blvd, you will receive your instructions upon arrival.*" Okay, then. And to think I had been looking forward to Vampire 101. I hated to admit that I was a little disappointed.

I tossed the phone in my bag and grabbed my essentials, then called out "I'm leaving!" to a probably still sleeping Mac. I headed out the door to the minivan and made a mental note to go car shopping soon so I could ditch the mom-mobile.

I arrived at the specified address twenty-five minutes later with Def Leppard blasting "Love Bites". I gawked for a moment before getting out of the van; the house was enormous. It was a large Cape Code with one and a half stories, a steep roofline, wood siding, and multi-pane windows, including the dormers. There was a large porch complete with white cushioned rocking chairs and potted flowers everywhere. It was gorgeous, and it told me that Nina Lambert was making some big bucks as Director of the Ministry of Vampire Affairs.

After ogling the house, I got out of the minivan, which looked even shittier to me in this posh environment. *Definitely* going car shopping soon, I thought. I headed to the front porch and rang the bell.

I wasn't sure what I expected, but I know I didn't expect Nina herself to answer the door. First, hadn't Doreen told me I would likely never see Nina in person? Second, what was the Director of the MVA doing answering her own door? Doesn't she have some sort of vampire butler? Maybe a ghoulish maid? A werewolf valet?

I stifled a giggle as Nina opened the door to allow me inside while keeping her distance from the light spilling into the entranceway. She was a tall, thin woman with pale skin and whiskey-colored eyes, just like Carl's and Alexandra's. Nina had her dark hair pulled back in a tight bun and she wore a burgundy twin set and cream-colored trousers. Doreen must have been right about Nina's age allowing her to stay awake longer; it was 8 a.m., and she showed no signs of fatigue.

"Cricket, so nice to meet you. I wanted to introduce myself in person on your first day," she said, extending her hand to me with a smile that didn't reach her eyes. I took it and tried not to recoil at how cold her skin was.

"Nice to meet you too, Mrs. Lambert," I said weakly. If everything I'd been told was true, an alpha predator stood before me. She could rip my throat out if she chose to and there would be nothing I could do about it. But it couldn't be true, right?

I followed her into the house where she stopped in the living room. It was an open floor plan which left part of the kitchen visible as well. If I thought the outside of the house was posh, the inside had it beat ten times over. There was plush carpeting in the living room and a gorgeous hardwood floor in the kitchen. Expensive looking heavy drapes hung over the windows, successfully blocking sunlight from entering the room. There was a big screen television hanging on the wall and flowers were in vases all around the room. A large couch with big fluffy cushions, antique tables and bookcases, and a large recliner rounded out the living area. There was also an enormous staircase that led in a spiral up to the second floor.

"Please, call me Nina," she continued as I tried not to stare in wonder at her home. I remembered what Doreen told me about some older vampires being able to read minds. I sure hope Nina is not one of them, I thought.

"In the future, your daily agenda will be waiting for you on the counter when you arrive. You may complete the day's tasks at your own pace, giving special attention to anything I have designated as a

47

priority. Here is a key to the house and a key to the black Mercedes in the garage, please use it to run errands." She handed me the keys and an envelope, which I opened while she spoke.

"Inside you will find a corporate credit card and MVA identification cards, should you be asked for ID. Please keep receipts for anything you charge and leave them on the counter on Friday afternoons." She indicated a basket on the marble kitchen counter.

She turned to face me then. "You should also know you may encounter my husband sometimes when you are here." She paused and looked at me with narrowed eyes. "He is human. Edward is in his seventies and in failing health. His nurses are in and out of the house as well." She stopped and seemed to wait for a reaction from me. It shocked me to learn that Nina's husband was an elderly human, but I kept my cool and remained unaffected by the news.

My lack of reaction seemed to please her; a small smile formed on her thin lips. She said, "Alright then, here is your list. Off you go. Call the office if you run into any problems as I am retiring for the day now." With that, she swept up the spiral staircase, and I was alone, wondering what the hell to do next.

I held the credit card and car keys in one hand and the list in the other. Right, I guess I should start by going over the list and choosing what to do first. Maybe I'll be delivering top secret documents to Russian spies. What if she wants me to bury a body for her or something? I'd have to draw the line there, I thought.

I sat down on the nearest chair and unfolded the paper which held my list. "Huh," I said aloud to no one.

Well, this was unexpected. I read the handwritten list to myself.

1. Pick up laundry detergent and paper towels at the grocery store
2. Pick up shipment of Perfect Plasma synthetic blood at Cleaners – 2 p.m.
3. Mail the package on the foyer table
4. Take Fluffy to the groomer

I stopped there. Fluffy? She hadn't mentioned a Fluffy. Who the hell was Fluffy and where was his or her groomer located? I pinched the bridge of my nose and sighed. I pulled out my cell phone and dialed.

"Doreen? I need help."

I arrived home that evening exhausted. It had been a tough day getting used to Nina's house, her car, her errands, and Fluffy. Doreen had thankfully come to my rescue and helped me find Fluffy, a 75-pound Golden Retriever, and haul him to his groomer. Fluffy hadn't been very cooperative, and I was now nursing a large cut on my forearm and several spots on my ass which were sure to bruise, thanks to Fluffy dragging me along in his efforts to avoid his bath. I was ready for a drink, a hot shower, and my bed, in that order.

I dragged my tote bag up the porch steps only to find Zeb sitting on the glider watching me with a small smile playing on his lips. He had two bottles of beer and held one out to me.

"Alright? Join me." He patted the spot next to him on the glider and I obliged, simply because the cold beer was exactly what I wanted at that moment in time. It had nothing to do with him looking extra hot tonight, I swear.

Dressed in a tight white t-shirt, ripped jeans, and boots, he looked good. His blond hair was in disarray and he was sporting a five o'clock shadow on his well-defined jaw. He was maddeningly sexy, and I really hated him for that. I should be mad at him right now for refusing to move out of Grandma's place so I could convince her to come back. I took a pull from the ice-cold bottle while he watched me, still smiling.

"So, how's the job working out?" he asked in that deep British accent, putting one ankle up on the opposite knee and leaning back.

I smirked. "Great, thanks for asking." I lifted my bottle in a cheers motion and took another pull. I looked away from him. "I talked to Grandma yesterday. She doesn't seem to know much about you. Why is that?" I turned to face him, meeting his eyes. It should be a crime for a man to have such piercing blue eyes, I thought as a shiver ran down my spine.

This time he looked away from me. "She didn't ask," he said, fiddling with the label on his beer bottle.

"Well, I'm asking. What's your deal, Zeb?" When I said his name, he met my eyes and I swear I felt a physical spark between the two of us. Nope, that just would not do, I thought, mentally locking Ho Cricket into a closet in the far reaches of my brain. You're supposed to be angry with him, Cricket, I reminded myself. Be angry.

He lifted his gaze to the sky, and the side of his mouth quirked upward. "My deal? I'm here for a job assignment, like I told you. And before you ask, no, I can't tell you what it is."

"Why not? Are you involved in the mafia? Is it drugs? All jokes aside, dude. I have a teenage daughter living here. I don't need anything going on that will put her in danger," I said, all traces of humor leaving my voice.

He met my gaze at that part about Mac. "Cricket, I would never stay here if it meant putting you or your daughter in danger. I hope you believe that," Zeb said earnestly.

I didn't know what to believe. I didn't really think he was in the mob or selling drugs, but who knew what he was up to? He wasn't being very forthcoming about his job situation or his background either, which was unsettling. How could I find out what he's up to? I wondered. As I pondered this, my gaze lingered on his tattoo sleeve. Up close it was even more beautiful, so intricate. The branches intertwined and wrapped around the scythe and it just seemed to go on and on. It was mesmerizing. Too late, I realized he had caught me looking.

He held his arm out further for my examination, smiling ruefully. "Like them?" he asked. I tentatively touched the scythe on his bicep, and I felt him tense.

"I do. They're beautiful. How long have you had them?" I asked as I traced a branch down to his wrist. "And why do you have a grim reaper's scythe among the leaves and branches?" His face darkened, and he retracted his arm out of my reach.

He was silent for a moment. "I don't like talking about the tattoos." Any trace of softness that had shown

51

in his eyes before vanished. Just like that, the moment was over.

I scoffed. "It seems you don't like talking about much of anything." I stood and deposited my empty beer bottle on the small table near the glider. "If you decide you'd like to talk, or better yet, find another place to live, let me know. Thanks for the beer."

He opened his mouth as if to say something, but I didn't give him the opportunity. I walked to my side of the duplex, went inside, and shut the door firmly. Yeah, I was being petty. The man was infuriating, being all sexy with those stupid pouty lips of his and not giving up any details about himself, his job, or his reason for being here.

Well, I had news for him. I would find out. I was a Daytime Concierge to the Director of the Ministry of Vampire Affairs in the Metro Nashville area. I still wasn't sure what that meant exactly, but there had to be some way I could use it to my advantage to find out what I wanted to know about Zeb Walker.

Chapter 7

The week continued in the same vein as my first day working for the vampires, pun intended. I continued to carry out the mundane, menial tasks that Nina assigned to me, such as emptying trash cans, picking up her groceries, delivering paperwork to other MVA associates, driving seventy-five miles to pick up a bottle of a specialty blood liqueur, and taking Fluffy for walks in the park. It was mind numbingly boring most of the time, but after seeing the automatic deposit that had shown up in my bank account this week from MVA, I figured I could handle a little boredom.

I came home exhausted from all the running around and spent my evenings at home, alone most of the time if Mac was at Luther's house, and falling asleep on the couch by 9pm. I hadn't even seen Zeb for several days and I hadn't been back to Forever Young to make another petition to Grandma about kicking Zeb out and coming home.

Finally, it was Friday, and I wanted to have some fun after my workday. I figured I had a right to celebrate literally surviving my first full week on the job working for a vampire. I dialed Doreen's number and asked her to meet me at The Rusty Nail at seven, to which she agreed excitedly. I checked in with Mac and she confirmed that she would be at Luther's, where his mother cared enough to cook a four-course meal for her family. It was precious that she still thought she could guilt trip me like that. I should send Luther's mother a thank-you card sometime, though.

I sat at the bar and made small talk with Joey for a bit while I waited for Doreen to show up. Joey told me about having to break up a fight earlier and how he had broken a guy's nose. After about thirty minutes of waiting, the sound of crickets chirping alerted me to a text message from Doreen.

Sorry hun, can't make it. Let's chat tomorrow! xoxo

"Crap," I said, tossing the phone on the bar. Joey moved back down to my end of the bar, refilling my shot glass while he was at it.

"What's wrong?" he asked, nodding to the discarded cell phone. "Did you get stood up?"

I blew out a sigh. "Yeah, looks like it. Damn it, I was looking forward to a fun night out too. Guess I'll head home and watch some Grey's Anatomy reruns until I fall asleep on the couch," I pouted.

Joey frowned. "I'm sorry, Cricket. If there was any way I could get away, I'd take you out to celebrate your first week on the job. You deserve it, you've been working hard. Hell, I've barely seen you in here this week," he said and winked at me.

"Well, I appreciate the thought, that's what counts, right?" I stood, adjusted my skirt, and looped my crossbody bag over my head.

Suddenly, I felt a little pissed off. Why should my night be ruined just because Doreen backed out on me? Screw it, I'll hit some bars on my own, find some live music to listen to, and maybe find someone new and interesting to flirt with while I was at it. Who needed Doreen anyway? I was a strong, independent woman for God's sake. I refused to go home and eat double mocha mint ice cream while drooling over McSteamy on Grey's until the wee hours of the night. I would take myself out for some fun, I decided.

However, I didn't say any of this to Joey because I knew he would try to talk me out of it, and he would probably succeed. So, I told him goodnight and quietly left The Rusty Nail. I stood on the sidewalk, looking up and down the street and trying to decide where I would go next.

Nashville was beautiful at night with all the neon lights and the Batman building towering above me on Broadway. I started walking towards the Riverfront; I figured there had to be some interesting bars down that way.

There were people everywhere and musicians at intervals on the street, playing to bystanders with guitar cases laying open in front of them to collect tips. It was loud and bright, and I was taking it all in when someone shoved me, and I nearly landed on my ass. Before I knew it, my assailant had cut the strap of my crossbody bag and was making off with it, leaving me stumbling and confused in his wake.

I righted myself as quickly as I could, then yelled, "Hey! Hey, that guy stole my purse!" I ran after him. Several people turned to stare but either determined that I was drunk or crazy, or possibly both, and none of them moved to help me. I looked around desperately, hoping to spot a police officer. Sure, there was always a cop around to catch you doing thirty-five in a twenty-five, but where were they when you needed them?

The guy was getting away, and I was getting winded trying to keep up with him. He was leading me away from Riverfront and I figured we were getting close to The Rusty Nail again. Just up ahead I saw something—or someone—bolt out of an alley and tackle my assailant to the ground. I slowed my pace and tried to catch my breath as I watched the attacker punch my mugger repeatedly in the face.

What is even happening right now? I was trying to comprehend the fact that I got mugged less than ten minutes ago and now my mugger was being assaulted. What are the odds? Hell, he deserved it though. As I came closer to the scene, and the men who were continuing to struggle with one another came into view, I gasped. What the hell was he doing here?

Zeb Walker, my sexy, secretive, asshole, biker neighbor was grappling with the mugger. Zeb had the guy in a headlock and then before I knew what had happened, Zeb had him face down on the sidewalk, hands restrained behind his back. Zeb was panting from the effort.

A crowd had gathered quickly; people were coming out of nearby shops and bars to have a look at what was causing the commotion. I pushed my way through the onlookers until I was standing right in front of Zeb and the mugger.

Zeb looked up at me, still breathing hard. "Alright, Cricket?" he said, still holding the struggling man down. Zeb was wearing what seemed to be his standard uniform, which was tight jeans, tight black t-shirt, black leather vest, and black boots. He looked damn good, with muscles bulging while he held the mugger down. If I wasn't so irritated and confused to see him here, I would have enjoyed the view.

My mouth was hanging open as I took in the scene before me. "No, not alright, Zeb. What the hell are you doing here? Wait. Were you following me?" I asked, thoroughly offended at the thought.

His face turned beet red. Son of a bitch, he had been following me. "Why would you follow me?" I demanded. Before he could answer, I walked over to where Zeb held the mugger down and I gingerly pulled my bag from his grasp.

"I loved this bag, by the way." I shook it by the cut shoulder strap in the mugger's face. His thin face went pale as he continued to struggle.

"Hey man, watch it! That hurts," the mugger said, still trying to free himself from Zeb's grip. It was no use; Zeb was about twice the guy's size. The mugger looked to be in his early twenties. He was thin, would've been tall had he been standing, and wasn't very attractive. I narrowed my eyes at him, then transferred my gaze to Zeb.

"Good thing I was following you, it would seem," Zeb said, still breathing heavily and meeting my icy stare. "You're welcome, by the way."

I took my cell phone out of the ruined bag and began dialing the non-emergency number for the Nashville police. "Nothing to see here folks, move along," I said to the gathered crowd who dispersed. "Boys, settle down. I'll have the cops here shortly and then," I pointed the phone at Zeb and glared at him, "you and I need to have a little chat."

We didn't have long to wait before the Metro Police showed up to arrest my would-be mugger, who's name turned out to be Chad. They took over restraining him, asked a million questions, and finally drove away with a scowling Chad in the back of the cruiser headed for a night in jail to await bail. I was honestly still shook; I wasn't sure what to make of it. It was quite an experience and one I'd rather not repeat.

When everyone had left, and it was just Zeb and I left standing on the sidewalk, I glared at him again. Okay, maybe he saved me, but still. I needed answers.

He turned to me and sighed. "We need to chat, Cricket." He ran his fingers through his disheveled blond hair and stood looking at me. "My bike's not far. Let's go find someplace private." Without waiting for my reply, he began walking down the sidewalk where I assumed his Harley was waiting somewhere in the shadows. I supposed that if I wanted answers, I had no choice but to follow.

We reached his bike, parked in an alley near where Zeb had caught Chad the mugger earlier. He retrieved a black helmet from the handlebars and tossed it to me, which I caught clumsily. "Put that on," he said before starting the engine.

I put the helmet on and tried not to think about how awful my hair would look when we reached our destination, wherever that turned out to be. Zeb revved the engine and looked at me, still standing on the sidewalk where I was adjusting the chin strap of the helmet. "Well? Let's go." He motioned for me to get on behind him.

Oh boy. I hadn't thought this through. This was a dangerous situation and I could already feel Ho Cricket demanding freedom from her prison cell. "This is fine," I whispered to myself and I walked over to Zeb and prepared to hop on the bike behind him. He flashed me a devilish smile and revved the engine again. Damn him. I glowered as I carefully climbed onto the bike and gingerly placed my hands on his back.

"Princess, you're gonna have to hold on tighter than that," he called over his shoulder as the bike lunged forward. My reflexes kicked in and I yelped, my arms seizing him around his waist tightly.

"Princess?" I yelled over the rumbling engine. I could feel his body shaking with laughter as we took off toward... where? I didn't know. I didn't really care at this moment either. He could drive me straight to hell on this Harley and I'd be ok with it. He smelled amazing, like leather and sandalwood. His ear was close enough to nibble on, if I had wanted to. Which I wanted to. Being in such close contact with him was doing funny things to my stomach, and other areas of my body.

I couldn't deny my attraction to him, even though it wasn't what I wanted. I wanted to be angry with him for not leaving when I had asked him to and for not answering my questions about his job. I wanted to be angry at him for following me tonight and because I didn't know why he would follow me in the first place. And for calling me Princess. I wanted to be angry that my rage was fading away the longer I sat on the back of this bike, holding on to him, feeling the heat of his body against mine.

About twenty minutes later Zeb was driving us into a parking lot at the marina. He parked the bike, and I clumsily heaved myself off the Harley and removed the helmet. He took it from me and hung it from the handlebars as I did the best I could to rearrange my hair. It was a cool night, especially here near the lake, and I missed the heat from his body. I mentally berated myself for that as I rubbed my arms.

Zeb turned to see if I was following and noticed me trying to warm myself up. He strode back to where I stood while removing the leather jacket he had worn for our ride; he slung it around my shoulders. "Come on," he said and motioned toward a bench near some slips.

I followed him and noticed there was hardly anyone around. There were many boats parked in their slips and I could hear the noise of people and music coming from the nearby restaurant, but he led us to a relatively deserted little area. I gathered my resolve; I would make him give me answers. We sat, and I turned my attention to him, determined not to let him distract me from finding out what the hell was going on.

"Explain," I said and waited, crossing my arms in front of myself.

He ran a hand through his hair and looked at me. "This will sound crazy; you understand?" he said, in that disarmingly sexy British accent of his.

"Crazier than having a mysterious neighbor who waters my plants and follows me around town in the middle of the night? Come on, Zeb. Just tell me what's going on. Who are you really?" I said, my voice sounding stronger than I felt. I suddenly wasn't sure if I wanted to know. Maybe, as they say, ignorance really is bliss? What if he told me he was a hit man, hired to kill me? No, that wouldn't explain why he's been watering the flowers, I thought. I turned back to him in time to see his lips quirk into a sad smile.

"I know you're working for Nina Lambert and I know she's a vampire. Not just any vampire either, she's the Director of the Ministry of Vampire Affairs. And you're in danger because of it," he said without

60

further ado. My mouth was probably hanging wide open. How did he know?

I gathered my wits once again; this was becoming a regular thing with me. "Wait. How do you know about the MVA and Nina? I mean, it's all crazy talk, right? They're pretending to be a vampire association, but none of it is real, right? They're paying me well for playing along. And what do you mean 'I'm in danger'?" I pulled his jacket tighter around me, suddenly feeling a chill deep in my bones.

Zeb smirked at me. "You think they're bantering you, that's it? I wish I could say you're right, but no, it's real. Vampires are very real, Princess."

I rolled my eyes. "Don't call me Princess. So, either you're also crazy or you're telling me I'm working for a real alpha predator. Are you going to tell me that Bigfoot is real too? How about Santa Claus, do you know him?" I said, still not buying it. I mean, come on. Not that working for bat shit crazy people who were pretending to be vampires was much better; it said more about me than them that I was willing to work for a bunch of mental patients. Mental patients who paid well, I added. Hey, I have bills to pay.

"They're real. I need you to understand that, Cricket. They are very real, and the Ministry is a dangerous organization. I know Nina only has you carrying out ordinary tasks now, but that will likely change soon. The organization I work for sent me here, in anticipation of that." He said, choosing his words carefully. He met my eyes, almost willing me to press him for more information. I could certainly oblige.

"Your *organization*? Why are they so concerned about little ol' me?" I asked, acerbically. Do I have a weird shit magnet attached to me somewhere? I mentally asked myself. I'd have to check my pockets when I got home.

He sighed and pinched the bridge of his nose. I was working his nerves, obviously. Good, I thought. "This is the really crazy part. Stay with me, here. I... am a Reaper," he said and cut his eyes at me, waiting for a reaction. I blinked a few times, and he seemed to take this as encouragement to continue. "Death, Inc. is my employer. The business front is a funeral home supply chain, but the real business is, well, death."

I was still listening intently, although I wasn't sure I was hearing him correctly. A *reaper*? This just keeps getting better and better. Maybe this was all a dream. Maybe I'd wake up soon and find that I was still a paralegal for Abernathy, Smith, and Sanchez and that vampires and reapers didn't exist.

"I didn't choose to become a Reaper. Let's just say it's my sentence for something that happened long, long ago and leave it at that for now," he said, running a hand through his disheveled hair. He looked at me with a slight grin and continued, "As I'm sure you know from folklore and movies, a Reaper's principal job is to collect the souls of those who have died and send them to their eternal resting place. Another lesser known part of my job is to keep people alive if it's not their time to die yet," he met my eyes again at that. "That's why I'm here, Cricket. For you."

I held his eyes for a few moments, speechless. Then I exploded.

"Cut the crap, Zeb. How dumb do I look to you? Oh wait, I can answer that. Dumb enough to buy this bullshit story you're feeding me right now? If you don't want to tell me who you are, that's fine. Keep your secrets. But please do not insult my intelligence like this." I began fumbling with my pockets, searching for my cell phone so I could call a cab to get me the hell out of here. I realized it was in my ruined bag, which was in Zeb's saddlebag on the bike. I stood and began marching off, I didn't know where I was going but I was getting away from this lunatic.

He was up and coming after me so fast I didn't realize it until he was gripping my elbow. He turned me around to face him. "It's true. It's true, I promise. I wish it wasn't, actually." He dropped my arm once I had stopped moving and took my hands instead. "My primary job here is to protect you. Taking a job with the MVA is equivalent to a lifetime assignment. You can't just quit. I'm sure they made you aware of that," he said, releasing my hands and putting his own on his hips.

"Well, I mean, that's what Carl said, but I didn't think he meant it. He meant it? And they're real?" I said, slowly and hesitantly, in a small voice.

"He did, and they are," he said sadly. "I know it's hard to accept and you probably still don't really believe it. You won't, for a while. Probably not until you witness something with your own eyes that makes it impossible to believe they're not real. But please don't let your guard down. My—bosses—have ways of detecting potential issues and that's when they send us out to do damage control. You're on their radar and you have to let me help keep you safe, okay?" He paused for a moment and then continued in his British cadence, "Besides, I have a 99% success rate, you don't want to muck that up for me."

I rolled my eyes. "Only 99%? That's not as reassuring as you think it is. What happened to the 1%?"

"That wasn't my fault and I can prove it," he said, his mouth twitching with the effort not to laugh.

"So, a Reaper, huh? Can you prove that?" I said jokingly, looking him up and down with narrowed eyes, still finding it hard to believe.

Zeb went silent while holding my gaze for a moment. Just as I was about to break eye contact from the discomfort of his intense stare, I saw his eyes change. It was as if a small flame was flickering behind his pupils, alternating shades of orange and red dancing in his eyes. As I stared—literally lost in his eyes—I felt the surrounding air growing warmer. I even heard the dry, hot air crackling all around me. After what felt like an eternity, he dropped my gaze and it was all over. His eyes were his usual sparkling, icy blue. The air temperature returned to normal and all I could hear were the sounds of music and people partying at the restaurant close by.

We stood silently for a few moments because after that demonstration and our earlier talk, I guess he'd shared as much as he was going to for now. I really didn't know what else to say either, after hearing everything he'd just revealed and seeing his transformation just now.

I broke the silence. "Alright, I've had enough supernatural revelations for one day. How about you just take me home now?"

Zeb's eyebrows shot up at that, so I added, "To *my* home, please," and punched his arm. I was so confused. Did I hate him or not? Was he insane? Was I insane? Was I lying in a coma somewhere hallucinating about working for vampires and having a Grim Reaper for a neighbor? I felt exhausted trying to sort it out; I just wanted to go to sleep and forget about it.

He stood with hands on hips, and his stance seemed to relax. He smiled with those kissable, pouty lips and breathed, "Right, I can do that." I went to remove his jacket, and he stopped me, "Keep it, it's freezing out here," he said.

I walked silently beside him back to the bike and got back on without too much awkwardness. I wrapped my arms around his middle again, and it seemed like such a natural gesture, even though it was only the second time in my life I'd ever done it. Yes, I was in danger alright, I thought. But I wasn't sure it was only the vampires that I should worry about as I relaxed into the heat radiating from Zeb's body and the bike took off, heading for home.

Chapter 8

I spent the rest of the weekend at home, watching the Twilight movies on repeat and eating ice cream. Mac was in and out, moaning about how there was never anything to eat in the house. I convinced her sit down and watch Breaking Dawn Part 2 with me though. We had a good time dissecting the various elements of what was believable and unbelievable, if vampires were real. For instance, would they really sparkle? We also debated whether Edward or Jacob was hotter. In the end, we settled on Jacob. If she only knew her mother was working for actual vampires, she'd be ecstatic, I thought. I made a mental note to find out if Carl or Nina sparkled. Overall, I just felt weird all weekend. My emotions were everywhere with anxiousness, dread, incredulity, and hunger all battling for first place. Seriously, I ate so much ice cream.

So, when I arrived Monday morning at Nina's place and she met me when I opened the door, I almost panicked and ran back to my van. She had a disapproving look on her face and I had a feeling that she was someone I didn't want disapproving of me.

Without a greeting, she said, "Cricket, why didn't you alert me that you were the victim of an attempted robbery the other night? Why am I hearing about this from other sources?" I entered the foyer where she stood well away from the sunlight filtering through the open doorway. She crossed her arms.

I awkwardly adjusted my bag on my shoulder and said, "Well, I didn't know I needed to?" I tried to keep the snarkiness at bay because I didn't want to give her a reason to literally rip my throat out now that I knew that was an actual possibility.

Her face softened a bit. "Darling, I was worried about you. And did you have any Ministry property with you at the time?" And there it was. She was wondering if I had anything of hers with me that the mugger could've stolen. I mentally rolled my eyes.

I forced a smile and said, "Thanks for your concern, Nina, I'm fine. And no, I wasn't on the job at the time, so I didn't have any MVA documents with me."

She studied me for a moment with narrowed eyes. She must have decided my not informing her was just a poor judgment call and not deliberate insubordination because she smiled, approached me, and gave me the coldest, most awkward hug I've ever received in my life.

"Well, thank goodness you're alright," she said, releasing me after a couple of seconds. I stood frozen, not knowing how to react to the completely unpleasant experience of being hugged by Nina Lambert.

She then gave me my list and bid me good day as she ascended the staircase where I assumed her bedroom was. Or her coffin? Hell, I didn't know. I sat down to read the list and Fluffy came bounding into the room and climbed up on the couch next to me. I petted his head as I went through the agenda and muttered to myself. Boring stuff. And Zeb was so worried about me being in danger. From the looks of it, a paper cut was the only thing I may be in danger of today.

I glanced at the stack of manila envelopes on Nina's dining room table. I was to deliver all of them to members of the MVA today, along with a few other mundane tasks. "So dangerous," I said to Fluffy and patted his head, to which he enthusiastically agreed by licking my arm.

I sighed and stood to retrieve the packets and be on my way when an elderly man with a walker came tottering into the room. I froze. This must be Edward, Nina's human husband who she had said was in poor health. I'd never met him before.

"Hello, Mr. Lambert?" I said, moving towards him with a hand outstretched. He was busy maneuvering the walker though, so I retracted my arm and made a move to help him.

"Ms. Jones, how nice to make your acquaintance," he said, moving surprisingly well for someone in failing health and had Hospice nurses with him round the clock. Speaking of which, where was his nurse now?

"Is there something I can help you with? Do you need me to get your nurse?" I asked, to which his face contorted into a frown. He stopped and met my eyes. He was in his seventies as Nina had said, very pale with paper thin skin, and hair that made him look like an albino troll doll. White tufts of hair stood up in all directions and he wore an expensive looking set of burgundy pajamas and a silk robe of the same color. Aging spots mottled his skin. I honestly couldn't picture him as Nina's husband and it probably showed on my face as he studied me, scowling.

"No, I don't need a damn nurse. I can get around on my own if they'd just leave me to it sometimes," he said in a gravely, parched voice, then continued on his journey to the sofa with his walker.

Okay then, cantankerous too. "Well, alright then. I'll just be going if there isn't anything you need." I stepped around him to retrieve the packets and be on my merry way.

"I said I didn't need a nurse, I didn't say I didn't need anything," he said, stopping at the sofa and setting the walker out of the way as he carefully perched himself on the couch. "Sit," he commanded. I didn't really care for his tone, but I obliged, not sure where this was going.

I waited for him to speak, which he did after a few moments of arranging himself comfortably on the sofa. "I need your help," he began, then stopped for a coughing spell. I waited it out, then he began again, "I need your help, Ms. Jones. I'll just get right to the heart of the matter. As you can see, I'm dying. I'm old, and I'm dying. My wife has wanted to turn me for years, but I've always refused; I don't want to live forever. And especially not at the age I'm at now." He stopped for another coughing spell, retrieving a handkerchief from his robe pocket and wiping his mouth with it.

"I'm done and I want to leave this world behind as quickly as possible," he continued after recovering and pocketing the handkerchief. "I've found someone who can facilitate this for me, but as I'm not able to get out and about, I will need some confidential assistance. I will make it worth your while to help me," he finished, and began coughing yet again.

I waited for him to finish and then said, "I don't know what I could do, that's not really part of my job, Mr. Lambert. Mrs. Lambert probably would..." I trailed off and he frowned and slammed his fist into the sofa with surprising strength for one who was dying.

Before he could say anything else, a dark-haired man dressed in scrubs entered the room and exclaimed, "Mr. Lambert! There you are!"

The nurse strode over to the sofa and urged Mr. Lambert to stand up, putting his walker in front of him. "Let's get you back to your room, shall we?" He gave me a smile that conveyed "I'm sorry" while Mr. Lambert grunted and jerked his arm out of the nurse's grasp.

As he conceded and allowed the nurse to lead him away, he turned to me and said, "We will speak again soon, Ms. Jones," giving me a piercing stare.

"Okay, bye," I said weakly, giving him a little wave. Well, that was weird. I quickly grabbed the packets I was to deliver for Nina and nearly ran out of the house before anything else could stop me.

After running all of Nina's errands for the day, I was heading home in the van when I heard crickets chirping. I had a text. I rolled my eyes; Mac told me she had changed it back. I glanced at my phone, mounted on the dashboard.

Hey girl, swing by the Nail on your way home!

It was a text from Doreen. I had been trying to contact her since the night of the attempted mugging when she had stood me up and I hadn't been able to reach her. I took the next exit and backtracked to the bar. I thought I might get her take on the almost mugging and Mr. Lambert's plea for help as well.

I walked in and immediately saw Doreen at the bar with two guys who were fawning all over her. She smiled and waved me over. She was wearing a hot pink jumpsuit and had used a crimping iron on her hair, which was in a side pony. Bright pink makeup and lime green jewelry completed her look. I just shook my head and smiled as I headed her way. Only Doreen could pull it off. I'd look like an overgrown Rainbow Brite doll if I tried it.

Joey caught my eye as I made my way to Doreen and he gestured as if to say, "give me a minute, we need to talk." That was a lot of information for one gesture, but that's what I took it to mean, anyway. Great, someone else wanted to grill me about the attempted mugging. Maybe I should compile a group text so that next time I got mugged I could let everyone in my life know at once. I mentally rolled my eyes as Doreen spotted me.

"Boys, my BFF is here, run along now! We have to catch up!" she said. I noticed one of them had the same whiskey-colored eyes that Carl and Nina had, so I immediately identified him as a vampire. He gave me a head to toe leer as he cleared out. Ewww.

I sat down at the booth opposite of Doreen and waited for it. She did not disappoint. "Girl! I heard about what happened, why didn't you call me?" She was vaping. Tonight it was Naked Unicorn. I didn't even want to know what that tasted like.

"Hello to you too. I tried, you didn't answer your phone. Didn't you see that you have voice messages?" I asked, a little snappier than I had intended. It was tiring, going over it with everyone over and over again. Grandma called yesterday to berate me for not calling her to say I was okay; news seems to travel fast on the Forever Young circuit. Then the thing with Nina this morning, now this with Doreen. And I spotted Joey heading our way as well. It was tedious. I'll just call a press conference next time.

"I saw those, but I had no idea it was so important!" Doreen exclaimed. How could she be so adorable and so maddening at the same time, I thought.

I didn't even attempt to hide my frustration this time. "Well try listening to them next time," I said, sighing as Joey sat down beside me in the booth.

He was looking good as usual. The dark curls at the nape of his neck were still wet from a recent shower, I assumed. That conjured up some mental images, let me tell you. His brown eyes met mine, full of concern. He put his arm around my shoulder and pulled me in for a quick hug.

"Cricket, I didn't hear until a few minutes ago or I would've come by your place to check on you. Are you okay? What happened?" He released me and I told my story as he and Doreen listened. I noticed Joey's jaw tense when I got to the part about Zeb popping out of the shadows to catch my mugger. Doreen, however, swooned upon hearing it.

"Oh Shug, I know being mugged was horrible, but that's so romantic how Zeb was there to save you!" She literally "squeed" and clapped her hands like a little girl. I laughed.

Joey huffed. "I wouldn't call it romantic. I'd say it was a little creepy. Does he just follow you around all the time now or what?" he asked, his face darkening. Quickly, he redirected the conversation and recovered himself.

"All I know is that if you're going to continue to work for that shady dry cleaning place doing God knows what, you need to protect yourself. That's why

I'm taking you shopping on Saturday. We're getting you some pepper spray, brass knuckles, and a stun gun. And you're getting a new car too, no more putting it off. Got it?" he said, pinning me with a determined stare.

Now that I thought about it, getting some self-defense equipment didn't sound like a bad idea. Based on what Zeb had said, which I wasn't about to share with these two, I may be in danger at some point so it would make me feel better to have some pepper spray on my key chain. And I'd been meaning to go car shopping anyway, so why not?

"That's a fantastic idea, Joey. Would you mind taking me shopping for that stuff? I'd have no idea what to get," I said, smiling and suddenly feeling much better. This would help me feel more secure and confident in my job. Pepper spray probably wouldn't do much to deter a vampire, but if I ran across anyone else like Chad the mugger, it could keep me safe. Speaking of vampires, I should probably ask Zeb if there was anything I could get to protect myself from them, too. Maybe I should wear a cross around my neck or carry a spray bottle of garlic juice in my bag? No, Doreen had said the garlic thing was false, I remembered.

"Of course, I don't mind. We'll make specific plans later this week, but it's happening on Saturday, okay?" He grabbed a long strand of my blonde hair that was hanging over my shoulder and gave it a gentle tug. He winked and said, "We have to keep our Cricket safe, right Doreen?"

Doreen raised her eyebrows and cut her eyes from Joey to me and back to Joey again. "Sure thing, stud," she said, watching him as he headed back to the bar. She looked back to me and grinned. "I think Joey has a thing for 'our Cricket'," she said, waggling her eyebrows and giggling.

I waved my hand, dismissing her, but mentally wondered if she was right. I mean, I had figured out that he probably had a little crush on me long ago, but was there more to it than that now? And if so, I wasn't sure if I was interested or not. He was my type on paper for sure. But I didn't know if it was worth risking a friendship for something that I wasn't even sure I wanted. I would have to file this in the "I'll think about it later" vault for the time being.

We had a drink and then talked for a while, giving me time to make sure I was okay to drive home. I decided not to bring up Mr. Lambert and what he'd asked of me. Maybe nothing else would come of it and it wouldn't even matter. And after telling her and Joey all about the mugging, she didn't seem to have much to say about that either. I assumed that if Chad's name had rung a bell or if anything about the mugging had sounded familiar to her, she would've said so already. I called it a night and headed home.

When I arrived, the lights were on in the house, so I knew Mac was home. Maybe she cooked some dinner, I thought, then realized that if she had cooked dinner, it was likely some sort of vegan dish which would disappoint the carnivore in me, anyway. As I climbed out of the van, I saw Zeb in the flower beds by my side of the porch. It struck me as hilarious that this big menacing biker dude, who I'd just found out was a Grim Reaper, liked to tend flowers.

"What is it with you and flowers, anyway?" I called to him, smiling and giving a little wave. He looked up and returned the smile. Tonight, he was wearing a blue flannel shirt, ripped jeans, and boots. He was also wearing black-rimmed glasses, which ironically made him look even hotter.

He smirked, standing up and replacing the water hose at the side of the house. "Well, you're not gonna water them, are you now?"

I rolled my eyes and flipped him a bird from where I stood at the porch. His grin widened at that. "I was about to have dinner, care to join me? I made my Nan's roast, you'd love it." He stood, waiting for my response. I had to admit, he looked adorable standing there in his flannel and glasses talking about his Nan's roast.

My mouth quirked up into a grin. "You cook, huh? I would never have guessed that. I suppose I should find out if Nan's roast is all it's cracked up to be then. Give me a couple minutes to change clothes and check in with Mac and I'll be right over," I said and disappeared into my side of the duplex to do just that. Is this a good idea? Ho Cricket answered with a resounding YES, but Conservative Cricket wasn't so sure. She was outvoted.

"Mac, where are you?" I called, throwing my bag on the couch and noticing the home remodeling show on the television. She came in from the kitchen carrying a large bowl of double mocha mint vegan ice cream. I had made sure to keep dairy free treats in the house for her since she started her vegan diet. Take that, Luther's mom.

She made a face when she saw me and then continued to sit in a nest of blankets and pillows on the couch.

"What's wrong? Fighting with Luther?" I sat down next to her and rubbed her leg, in what I meant as a comforting, motherly, gesture. She grimaced.

"Yes. And stop doing that," she said, taking a bite of ice cream and turning to the tv. Chip and Joanna were about to show us how to update an outdated ranch house, and Mac was more interested in that than she was in talking to me. Typical.

Long ago I had accepted the fact my sweet little girl, who had hung on every word I said and had loved being showered with hugs and kisses, had been replaced by this angsty teenager. I sighed. That's just the way it was with most mothers and daughters. I remembered behaving the same way with my mother. Paybacks were hell, I thought.

I wondered what poor Luther had done to deserve the wrath of Mac. I hoped he was making reparations at this very moment, not only for his sake, but for mine. She'd be hell to live with until they had made up, I thought.

"Well, it looks like you've got your evening sorted, so unless you want to talk about it, I'm going next door to have dinner with Zeb," I said and waited for it. She cut her eyes at me, and then promptly rolled them.

Before taking another bite of double mocha mint, she said, "Wow, mom. You don't waste any time."

"What's that supposed to mean? It's just dinner. And he's our neighbor, I'm just being neighborly." I said, rationalizing.

"Fine. Just make sure you're being neighborly with a condom. I don't need a baby brother or sister to share the inheritance with," she said, once again rolling her perfectly lined and smoky eyes at me while judging me with teenage contempt.

"It's just dinner, Mac," I said, swatting her leg and leaving her to it. God bless Luther's soul for putting up with this one, I thought, and said a quick prayer that he'd be back in her good books again soon. I headed upstairs to get changed.

Twenty minutes later, I was standing in front of the other door of the duplex, wearing a light blue floral top and jeans, with my hair pulled back into a ponytail. I hated to arrive empty-handed, so I had a package of Oreo cookies with me that I had found in the pantry. I was second guessing my judgment on the Oreos and was about to chuck them into the bushes when the door opened. Zeb had a dish towel thrown over his shoulder, which made for an interesting, but hot, domestic picture of him. He still wore the flannel and glasses and the aroma of the roast wafted past him, making my mouth water.

"Come on in." He grinned and moved aside to allow me inside. He spotted the Oreos and looked at me questioningly.

I bit my lip. "I brought dessert," I said weakly, and he laughed.

"My favorite. How did you know?" He winked and took them from me, placing them on the kitchen counter.

"Lucky guess," I said and looked around. Grandma's furniture was still here, but the place looked completely different. The room was in disarray, and

Grandma would have a fit if she could see it. Blankets and pillows strewn about, flannel shirts thrown over the back of the couch, water bottles and coffee mugs abandoned in various places. I stifled a giggle thinking about Grandma's reaction. Maybe I should just snap a few photos to show her. She'd be ready to toss Zeb out and move back home in a heartbeat, I thought. That was exactly what I had wanted a week ago, but now, here I stood with this man. He had come to my rescue, albeit with questionable tactics, which he had explained with a questionable story. Yet I felt like I could trust him. And the thought of Grandma deciding to move back home and kicking Zeb out right now surprisingly made me feel a little sad.

"Have a seat there on the couch, I'll get you a drink," he called from the kitchen. I moved a flannel out of the way and sat down as he came in and handed me a beer. He sat down next to me and smiled.

"So, how's work going?" he asked. I was about to answer when I remembered what Mr. Lambert had asked of me and wondered if I should mention it to Zeb. Maybe I should. I mean, he's supposed to be my Fairy God Reaper or something, so he would probably want to know. But then again, do I want to give him even more reasons to follow me around everywhere?

I smirked. "You mean you don't know? Weren't you following me today? Laying down on the job, Zeb?" I nudged him with my elbow and his face went red. I figured I'd let him off the hook. "It was weird. Every day working for Nina is its own special kind of weird, you know? Today I had to deliver a bunch of packets to MVA officials and before that, I finally met

Mr. Lambert at the house. Do you know about him?" I asked, taking a pull from my beer.

Zeb nodded. "Yeah, a right old fellow, human. An odd pairing, eh?"

"Right. And he's not well. In fact, he's dying, and he wants to speed that process along. His nurse interrupted him, but I believe he was trying to ask for my help with that," I said, fiddling with the label on my beer.

Zeb pinched the bridge of his nose, closed his eyes, and sighed. "What did you say?"

I scoffed. "Well, I didn't get the chance to answer because his nurse walked in and interrupted us, but I was about to tell him no," I said. "It's so weird. Why wouldn't he have let Nina turn him years ago?" I mused, turning to look at Zeb.

He had a worried expression. "Let me do some research on those two. Don't do anything and don't tell anyone else," he said.

"I wasn't going to. I only told you because, well, it seemed like I should," I said, curtly. It annoyed me that he thought I might help Mr. Lambert off himself. I would apparently do a lot of things for money, like menial chores for alpha predators, but I had a line I wouldn't cross. I rolled my eyes at him.

"I'm glad you told me, Princess. Now, how about we eat?" He rose from the couch with that and I followed him to the dining room where he had a couple of place settings ready. The roast smelled amazing and I couldn't wait to tuck into it. We ate, talked, laughed, and drank. A lot. Good thing I didn't have to drive home, I thought. I only had to stumble next door and hope Mac was asleep when I got there.

I told him about meeting Doreen at The Rusty Nail and that Joey wanted to take me shopping for some self-defense equipment. "That's such a good idea, right? I hadn't even thought about it, but it would be good to have some pepper spray," I said, finishing the last bite of roast on my plate.

Zeb frowned and raised his eyebrows. "Well yeah, but does he really know what he's talking about?" Hmmmm. I thought I was detecting a little jealousy here. Interesting development.

"What's there to know? Pepper spray is pepper spray, right? Unless there's something I should get specifically for deterring vampires?" I asked. I finished my latest bottle of beer and noticed my head was feeling a little fuzzy.

His face brightened at that. "Yes, actually. I'll get you a few things, tell Joey not to worry about it," he said and went back to finishing his roast. I smiled to myself. Bingo. He's jealous. On one hand, it made me feel kind of good that he was jealous of me spending time with another man. On the other hand, it was kind of not his business, and I was a little irritated. So, I pressed on.

"Okay, I'll let him know. But he wants to take me to look for a new car too, so we'll probably just do that instead on Saturday." I smiled sweetly.

His smile faltered, and I stifled a giggle. This was fun. "Oh. A new car, eh? What's wrong with your van?" he asked, trying to be nonchalant.

"Aside from the fact that it's twenty years old? Isn't that enough? And I can afford one now, with all this bank I'm making from the vamps." I winked and stood to clear the table, but he stopped me.

"Nope, sit down. I've got it. Want another beer?" He asked, gathering up our dishes. Wow, he cooks, and he does dishes too? Be still my heart, I thought.

We eventually wound up back in the living room with our drinks. The lights were dim and at some point he must have lit a few candles, which were twinkling and casting a golden glow over the room. We sat closer together on the couch this time and he caught me admiring his tattoos again. "So, tell me about these. Do they have anything to do with your job as a Reaper?" I reached out and traced the curve of the scythe on his bicep. His muscles tensed under my touch.

"Yeah, actually they do. This sounds crazy, but they hold magic." He held his arm out and looked at them too, like he was seeing them for the first time. As we watched, I swear I saw some movement in the tattoos. The branches swayed like a breeze was blowing them, but the motion stopped as quickly as it began. Maybe it was just the beer playing tricks on my mind, I thought. Or was it the magic he spoke of?

"I can't remember a time when I didn't have them," he said, turning his arm back and forth so I could get a better look.

"What does the magic in them do?" I asked, taking another drink of my beer.

Zeb gave me a look, probably trying to decide if I was being serious or snarky about the magic. He must have determined I was genuinely interested. "Well, they alert me to imminent deaths in my vicinity and I use the magic in them when it's time to collect souls. They also serve to keep track of the remaining time I have left as a

Reaper," he said, his voice sounding a little sad as he continued looking at his tattoos.

I thought I'd try to steer the subject in another direction, hopefully a happier direction. "So where are you from? What brought you here? I mean, besides me and my future shenanigans?" I winked at him. I really had wondered about where he was from and how he had wound up in America. I was curious about how he became a Reaper too, but I remembered him saying something about it being some sort of "sentence" once before and with the way he got all sad just now, I figured maybe now wasn't the best time to ask about that.

"I'm from Chatham, England. I haven't been there in a long time though. A really long time," he said, and then turned to me. "And as for what brought me to America from England, well, let's just say it's a long story. Probably best kept for another time." His mouth quirked up into a somber smile.

Not quite an open book, is he? Why was he so sexy and infuriating at the same time? I wondered. It was like pulling teeth to get information out of him. Still, I'd take what I could get when I could get it.

"Alright. Well, on that note, I guess I should get home. Mac is probably wondering what's keeping me." I smiled and rose to go.

He rose with me, took a step closer and then his hand was at the back of my neck, pulling me towards him. Zeb's mouth was on mine, kissing me softly and cautiously at first. He pulled back and looked at me as if to gauge my reaction and after a couple moments, I grabbed the flannel he was wearing with both hands and pulled him back to me.

I had my hands in his hair as our lips met again, this time not so softly. His arms went around my waist, pulling me closer to him. Zeb held me tight as his hands moved up my back and under my shirt, sending tingles down my spine as we continued to kiss. I caught his bottom lip in mine and gave it a little nip, eliciting a low growl from him as my hands wandered down his muscular biceps and then back up his chest. I felt his warm hands cupping my face and then his fingers were running through my hair. He kissed me softly once more before finally breaking away.

"Wow," I whispered as he leaned down, touching his forehead to mine. That had been one great kiss. Not that I had a lot to compare it to since my divorce eighteen months ago, but I felt confident in saying it was among my lifetime top five kisses. Shivers were still running through every cell in my body.

He met my eyes and smiled at me. "Yeah," he breathed. We stayed like that for a few moments more, then I remembered I had been about to go home.

"So, I'll see you later? Probably tomorrow, right? Since you live next door to me," I babbled, backing towards the door as his lips twitched with the effort of not laughing.

"Right. Sleep well, Cricket." He said as I shut the door behind me and fumbled my way over to my side of the duplex in the dark, with his kisses still lingering on my lips.

Chapter 9

The next morning, I arrived at Nina's a little early. I had an appointment later in the afternoon so I figured I could get a head start on whatever boring tasks I'd be doing today, like taking Fluffy to have his nails trimmed, picking up toilet paper at the grocery, or taking her expensive suits to the tailor. It was tedious, but it paid well, so I made sure my playlist and wireless ear buds were ready to go so I could just get it done.

I used the key Nina had given me to unlock the door, and I crept inside to the dining room where she always had my instructions waiting. I stopped halfway there though; I heard noises coming from the living room. Because I'm nosy, I tiptoed my way over to the entranceway and then hid myself behind a large potted plant.

It was Nina and another young male vampire—I knew because of the pale skin and the whiskey-colored eyes. They were with what appeared to be a human female. She was sitting on the couch next to Nina in the unlit room. They had all been laughing amongst each other but now the blonde human girl, dressed in a skimpy cocktail dress, pulled her hair to the side and presented her neck to Nina. I saw Nina's gaze go to the girl's neck. She smiled seductively and her fangs dropped. I gasped and quickly put a hand over my mouth. My eyes were probably as big as saucers as I watched Nina latch onto the girl's neck to feed.

I stood motionless, not sure what to do next. Do I stay here until they're done? Do I squeeze my eyes shut and pretend I never saw this? The man and the—blood donor—continued to make small talk while Nina drank. The girl was used to this I realized. She wasn't afraid, and she wasn't resisting. Still, I felt weird. I wanted to be anywhere but here right now. I turned to creep back to the dining room when I heard the male vampire speak.

"So, Nina, how many more days do we have left?" he asked as she finished drinking from the girl and gingerly wiped her mouth with a white linen handkerchief.

Nina smiled as she looked at him. She waved her hand to dismiss the girl who grabbed her purse and exited by a door on the opposite side of the room. My attention went back to Nina. Her fangs had retracted by now.

"Aaron, you know we have exactly one week left to keep your father alive. Just one more week."

Aaron, who I now recognized as a younger, handsomer version of Edward Lambert, appeared to be a little younger than me. He had those vampire eyes though, so who knew how long he had actually been in his late twenties. He had short brown hair and was tall and lean.

"Good. I don't think I could bear a day more," he said as he poured them both a glass of champagne and brought Nina's to her on the couch.

"I agree. I hope Edward's little game has amused him all these years he's been playing with us. It's all about to end and I'm glad of it. Why didn't he let me turn him years ago when he was young and virile? Now he's old, and he wants to die so badly. And he wants to cheat me out of what is mine. I earned it, damn it. It's been so many years and now he wants to stop me from having what I've worked for. I won't let it happen, Aaron." She rose and paced the room as she spoke.

It kind of reminded me of a scene from a soap opera, honestly. I just needed a close-up of her face in anguish with Aaron standing idly behind her to make it complete. I stifled a giggle. Cricket, this is not the time, I chastised myself.

As if on cue, Aaron walked up behind Nina as she turned to face him. She sat the champagne glass down on the nearest table and took his face in her hands. Then she kissed him, deeply and urgently. His hands went to her hips as he kissed her back.

This was too real for me suddenly. I'd just witnessed Nina drinking from a live blood donor and heard some vague stuff about Edward that could probably get me killed, or at least mildly tortured, if Nina knew I'd heard any of it. Not to mention, I'd just watched her kiss her own stepson, which was gross.

On tip toes, I crept slowly and quietly back to the dining room where I could happily retrieve my list of mundane tasks and be on my merry way. As I was sticking envelopes and folders into my messenger bag, I heard footsteps behind me.

"Cricket. What are you doing here so early?" It was Nina, standing at the doorway I'd just been snooping at. She narrowed her eyes and waited for an answer.

"Oh, Nina, hello. I need to knock off an hour early this afternoon, so I'm just getting a head start on the day," I said, a little too cheerfully. "I have a dentist appointment later." I added, trying to sound cool. I thought I was pulling it off. She eyed me suspiciously for a moment, looking me up and down. Did she know I'd overheard her talking to Aaron and seen their kiss?

"Well, have a wonderful day," she finally replied curtly, turned on her heel, and left. I released a massive breath I hadn't realized I was holding. Right, I thought. I had to get out of there immediately. I finished gathering what I needed and left as quickly as I could.

The rest of the week passed uneventfully for the most part. Mac and Luther had made up (thank God), and she was back to her usual angsty, lovable self. Grandma was still living at Forever Young with Gus, and I'd stopped by for another visit. I'd found Grandma taking a hot yoga class, along with most of the other elderly ladies at the center. She claimed it had nothing to do with the young, fit, male yoga instructor who came to Forever Young weekly to teach them hot yoga. She said she only took the class because hot yoga removed impurities from one's system. I, however, knew better. Where do you think Ho Cricket came from? It was in our DNA. I still never met Gus, which I was beginning to think was a carefully orchestrated avoidance maneuver on Grandma's part. She was probably afraid of what I might say to him. Can't say that I blame her.

I hadn't seen much of Zeb all week either, just once or twice in passing on the porch. I still felt a little awkward seeing him after our kiss the other night at his place. There was an attraction there, no denying it. In fact, that was the understatement of the year. But I hadn't dated anyone since the divorce from John-Clarke was final, almost eighteen months ago, and as much as my hormones wanted to go full speed ahead, my brain wanted to slow down. I wanted to know more about Zeb, and I guess I was feeling a little shy too, now that our mutual attraction was out there. Gah, why did Logical Cricket have to stick her nose into everything?

Before I knew it, Saturday had arrived and Joey was on my doorstep, ready to take me car shopping. I answered the door in a short, burgundy dress with a large floral pattern on it, and a mustard-colored cardigan. I had scraped my long blonde hair back into a ponytail and I had a brand-new cross body bag to replace the one Mugger Chad had ruined. With a travel coffee mug in hand, I was ready to go.

"Hey Joey!" I greeted him as I opened the door. He smiled at me, and I noticed him giving my long, bare legs a double take. Yeah, this momma's still got it.

I turned to lock the door behind me since Mac wasn't home and heard a gruff, British voice coming from behind me.

"How's it going, mate?"

It was Zeb. I bit my lip. I hadn't really thought this through, having Joey pick me up here at the house. But... this could work to my advantage, I thought. I spun around and pasted a bright smile on my face.

"Hey Zeb! This is my friend, Joey, remember I told you about him the other day? Joey, this is my neighbor and friend, Zeb." I hurried through the introductions and stood back to observe. The men sized each other up, each with some variation and mixture of confusion and concern etched across their faces.

Joey recovered first and took a step towards Zeb, reaching his hand out. "Hey, man." Zeb shook his hand and nodded.

Zeb was wearing another flannel, jeans, and his black-rimmed glasses. Looking adorably nerdy for a tough biker. He crossed his arms over his chest and said, "Heading out?" His expression was cool and collected.

"Remember, I told you that Joey and I are going out car shopping," I said, dropping my keys and phone into my purse. Joey nodded in agreement and stood with hands in his pockets. He was also in jeans, a tight-fitting black t-shirt, and his unruly dark curls were just touching the collar of his shirt. Well built, maybe not as muscular as Zeb, and no tattoos. At least not visible ones.

"Oh yeah. I remember that. Well, good luck then," Zeb said and turned his back to us and continued fiddling with the garden hose. I raised my eyebrows. "Good luck then"? Well, I'm not sure what I expected exactly, but that wasn't it. Especially not considering our recent lifetime top five kiss.

Joey smiled and indicated that we should go. He headed down the stairs toward his truck in the driveway. I followed slowly while watching Zeb ignore us, and feeling annoyed at that. I mean, what girl doesn't enjoy a little jealousy once in a while? And I could understand him not wanting to act jealous, but this blatant display of not giving a shit was taking things a little too far. I let my hand drag the banister as I descended the stairs.

"Okay then… see you later," I said, still watching him. By now, Joey was already behind the wheel of the truck and starting the engine.

Just then, Zeb turned to me and held my gaze for a moment. In the space of about half a second, the corner of his mouth quirked up into a grin and he winked at me, then turned back to the garden hose. If I had blinked, I would've missed it. But oh, how glad I was that I hadn't blinked. I smiled to myself and hurried out to join Joey in the truck, with butterflies doing backflips in my belly.

After a few hours of haggling with a salesman named Dale at Nashville Motors, Joey had helped me negotiate a decent deal on a brand-new Nissan. It was black and shiny and had all the bells and whistles. I was in love. I couldn't wait to show Mac and tell her that if she wanted it, the old van was hers. Knowing her, she'd say the minivan was "vintage" and her little hipster black heart would be thrilled.

As I pulled into the driveway, Joey's truck pulled in behind me. I had told him there was no need to follow me home, but he had insisted. I scanned the house and yard and saw no sign of Zeb. His bike was gone too. I got out of the car and admired it for a moment, smiling. I turned, and Joey was standing next to me, looking at me and smiling.

"I had fun with you today, Cricket," Joey said, shoving his hands into his pockets. "We should hang out more often, and not just at The Nail," he said with a grin.

"I had a great time too. Thanks for making me go car shopping finally. I would've put it off forever," I said. "And for helping me get such a deal, too. You gave that salesman a run for his money, Mr. Morley." I flashed him another smile. I dug around in my purse for my keys, since the house showed no signs of Mac being in there.

When I looked up, Joey was in front of me, one hand resting on my hip and the other tilting my chin up so I was looking at him. The keys slipped from my grasp and hit the ground. Then he kissed me. His lips brushed mine, slow and soft as my heart began fluttering in my chest. I closed my eyes and relaxed as his arms encircled my waist and pulled me closer. A warm tingly sensation spread throughout my body while his hand ran up my spine and found its way to my hair. Joey's lips were soft, and the masculine scent of his cologne surrounded me. Finally, he pulled away and stepped back, letting his hand graze my arm as he did.

"Cricket, I had a great time with you today. I mean it." He squeezed my hand, then let it drop. I think I had sudden onset paralysis because I wasn't sure what my face was doing at that moment and I couldn't speak. Was this real life? Was this happening to me? Not one, but two hot guys had kissed me within the space of a week. Hashtag blessed.

Joey smiled and said, "See you soon?" to which I could only nod in agreement before he was back behind the wheel of his truck. I watched him drive away and after a moment, I remembered to retrieve my keys from the ground.

I wasn't sure how I felt about that kiss. That amazing kiss. Or how I felt about Joey. Or Zeb. There was no doubt about it, I was attracted to both men. I would have to process my emotions over wine and trash tv for the rest of the evening, I decided as I went inside and closed the door behind me.

Chapter 10

I invited Doreen over the next day to hang out and chit chat. Sadly, I didn't have that many female friends in my life, so I thought I'd try to turn Doreen into one. Sure, she was older than me and we didn't have much in common. Except working for alpha predators, which was a pretty big common factor. And she was easy to talk to and non-judgmental. So, she was the perfect person to discuss the Zeb versus Joey situation with. I figured I'd also get her take on Nina and whatever was going on at her house.

We sat in my living room with glasses of wine and the Ed Sheeran station playing on Spotify in the background. Mac was at Luther's house, big surprise, and I hadn't seen Zeb all day.

"Ooh I love this song," Doreen said when "Shape of You" started playing. She was wearing a purple jumpsuit today with animal print heels. With her hair pulled into a high pony and wearing oversized gold hoop earrings, I felt underdressed sitting next to her on the couch in my own home. Maybe I should've dressed up a bit, I thought as I looked down at my jeans and sweatshirt that read "but first, coffee".

"So, you've never said, Doreen. Are you seeing anybody?" I topped off my wine glass and sat back, putting my feet up on the coffee table.

She laughed. "I've always got one or two on the hook, babe. Life's too short not to. So, what about you and the bartender, Joey?" she asked, waggling her eyebrows at me and taking a sip of wine.

"He took me car shopping yesterday," I said. She looked at me and waited for more. "We kissed."

She nodded, smiling. "But I'm not sure I want to go there, you know? We're friends. Plus…" I trailed off.

"What? Honey, Joey is hot, and he's a sweet guy," she said, taking another sip of wine.

I swirled the wine in my glass and nodded. "He is. There's someone else I'm attracted to also. It's confusing." I suddenly didn't want to talk about it anymore, and I wasn't sure why. Maybe I was afraid of the advice she would give me.

"Oh, a love triangle! Those are amazing," Doreen said, sipping her wine and bouncing her leg to the music.

Right, so maybe she wasn't the perfect person to discuss this with after all, I thought. I changed the subject.

"Do you know Edward Lambert's son, Aaron, by chance? I overheard him with Nina on Friday. They were having a weird conversation. What's the scoop on that family?" I poured more wine in her glass as I spoke.

"Oh, yeah… so I heard that Nina and Edward met in the early 80s. He was already middle aged at that point and she was hundreds of years old, but he and Nina fell in love. I guess she thought he'd eventually let her turn him. But he never did. Aaron is his son from a previous marriage. Aaron begged Nina to turn him when he was in his late twenties," she paused and took a drag from her vaping device. Pink Lemonade, I noticed.

"So," I said, quickly trying to do the math in my head, "Aaron got turned in the early 2000s then? Still doesn't look a day over twenty-eight and he doesn't even have to moisturize, lucky him," I said, sipping my wine.

She nodded and continued. "Edward was completely against it though, and he was furious when he found out what Nina did. Their relationship never recovered from it, but they stayed married. It was mutually beneficial. He had all the money, and she had all the connections. Edward is worth a fortune now, and I heard that awhile back he had a witch cast a spell. Or a curse? Whatever you want to call it," she said, waving a hand dismissively and exhaling vapors away from my general direction.

I nearly choked on my wine. "Wait, a curse? And witches are a thing?" I said in disbelief. I guess I shouldn't be surprised after what I've witnessed already. Hell, I'm working for vampires and living next door to a Grim Reaper. Nothing should surprise me at this point. But it did. What else was out there that I didn't know about yet?

Doreen giggled. "Oh honey, yes. Nashville is full of them, but most of them are young around here. It's the old ones you want if you want something complicated and you want it done right. Anyway," she continued, "this curse or spell, it said that Edward had to die of natural causes after his seventy-third birthday. If Nina or anyone else turned him, or if he died before then, Nina and Aaron would get none of his fortune. And the kicker? They'd also become mortal again." She concluded with a shrug.

"Wow. That's unbelievable," I said, processing this new information and what it meant considering recent conversations I'd had and overheard.

"I mean, I don't know if that's true. But that's the word on the street," she said and polished off her glass of wine. She then asked to use my bathroom before I could say anything else. I pointed her down the hall to the right and pondered what she'd said.

Nina had said they had one week. Did that mean that Edward was about to turn seventy-three in one week and after that, she'd be free to kill him? What about Edward, he'd asked me to help him contact someone to help him commit suicide now. So, he wanted to activate the curse, if there actually was one? Hell, were witches even real or was Doreen just telling tales? Add that to the list of things to ask Zeb, I thought.

Did Edward hate Nina so much for turning his son that he would have a witch curse her with mortality? And I wondered, why the age of seventy-three? How was that significant? This whole Nina, Edward, and Aaron situation was weird. I decided to file it away for additional thought when I was much more sober, possibly tomorrow. And it would give me a decent excuse to talk to Zeb also.

Doreen came out of the bathroom and announced that one of her guys had texted her and wanted her to stop by on her way home. Also known as "the booty call". I teased her a bit and sent her on her way, noticing a sleek black Porsche in Zeb's driveway, parked next to his bike, as Doreen left. Interesting, he never has company, I thought.

I stood on the porch watching Doreen's compact car back out of the drive when Zeb's door opened and out came a tall, thin woman, dressed in a black spandex mini skirt and crop top. She had long, straight platinum blonde hair with purple tips, floral tattoos on her legs, and black lipstick. She carried a large black tote decorated with fringe and silver buckles. She turned to descend the porch stairs and saw me. My eyes were probably as big as saucers. She stopped and smiled at me.

"Oh, hello there. You must be Cricket. Sebby has told me so much about you," she said in an Australian lilt, stepping towards me with one hand reaching out. Her eyes were green, and her skin was so pale it resembled porcelain. She was gorgeous. And what the hell was she doing coming out of "Sebby's" place?

I recovered myself as quickly as I could and shook her outstretched hand. "Yes, hi, I'm Cricket. And you are…?" I trailed off. Funny, he's told her all about me, but he hadn't said a word to me about this Australian goddess on our mutual porch.

"Esmeralda. My mates call me Essie. I'll answer to either," she said, laughing. "Listen, I've gotta run now. It was nice meeting you, ta ta," she called over her shoulder, descending the stairs and heading for the Porsche.

"Ta ta," I said weakly, watching her go. Well, that was disappointing, I thought, feeling my heart sag in my chest. But I have no claim on him, we were only just getting to know one another, and we've only shared the one lifetime top five kiss so far. I mean, how was this any different from me flirting with Joey, Logical Cricket pointed out. Probably for the best anyway, she continued. Do we really want to get involved with a Grim Reaper? How would we explain that to the grandkids one day? "Kids, Grandpa's gonna miss your

soccer game today, he has to go collect some souls."
Probably wouldn't go over very well, Logical Cricket
said.

She had a point, but I still couldn't help feeling
let down. It had felt good thinking he was into me and
now that I had met Essie I had to admit she was so
completely his type on paper… how could I ever
compete with her?

I heard some noise coming from Zeb's place
and instantly decided I didn't want to talk to him right
now. I was still processing Essie and how I felt about
Zeb, her, and even Joey, so I dashed back inside and
shut the door quietly behind me. I peeked out my
window to see Zeb open the door and look around, his
gaze pausing on my door. I drew back quickly; I was
afraid he'd see me. Guess I would go drown my
sorrows in double mocha mint chocolate chip ice cream
and fall asleep to some old Buffy the Vampire Slayer
episodes.

Chapter 11

The next day, I went to work as usual, picking up my list and instructions and various packages for delivery from Nina's dining room. All was quiet in her house, and I was glad. There were a ton of folders and envelopes today, each with an address showing where it should go. I popped my wireless ear buds in and turned on some Led Zeppelin to get in the mood for a long day in the car.

After a few deliveries and pickups, I decided I could use an iced coffee. I pulled in at Starbucks, locked Nina's car up, and headed in. And who did I see when I walked in besides my favorite bartender. He hadn't spotted me, so I walked up behind him in line and casually bumped into him.

"Hey Joe, are you lost?" I said as he turned to see who had smacked into him. His face broke into a grin when he saw me.

"Cricket!" he exclaimed and pulled me into a hug. He smelled like soap, all fresh and clean. He was not looking the part of bartender today, dressed in khaki slim fit pants, a tan and black striped sweater, and tan suede oxfords. He cleaned up nicely, I thought, admiring this unusual view of Joey.

"Khaki's and oxfords? Fancy. Where are you off to?" I said as we moved forward in the line. Joey blushed.

"Birthday party later in Kentucky. Grandma is turning ninety-three. We have a huge party every year for her birthday because she keeps reminding us it could be the last one." He smiled and rolled his eyes.

I laughed. "I think I'd like her," I said. The line moved again, and I started mentally putting my order together. Venti iced coffee, extra cream, four pumps vanilla, three stevias. And a cake pop.

Joey's face fell. "I would've asked you to come, but I didn't think it was something you'd be into. But maybe next year," he said, smiling at me.

I grinned back. We finally reached the front of the line and Joey ordered and then said, "Hers too," nodding in my direction, so I thanked him and added my order to his.

After a little more small talk about the party, his grandma, his extended family in Kentucky, and the bar, our drinks were ready.

"Well I guess I'd better get back on the road," I said to Joey. He locked eyes with me and with his free hand, he let his fingers graze all the way down my arm until it reached my hand, which he squeezed before letting go.

"See you soon?" he said, to which I nodded with a smile. He left while I stayed behind to grab a few napkins. I had a cake pop to eat, and it was gonna be messy.

I headed out the door with my treats in hand, turned the corner and saw someone closing the passenger side door of Nina's car. He was tall, thin, and wore jeans, a white t-shirt, and a red baseball cap. He glanced around to see if anyone was watching and then took off.

"Hey! Stop, what are you doing?" I yelled, making a run for the car and whoever this guy was. He didn't turn around; he just ran faster until I finally lost sight of him. I went back to the car and examined it. No signs of forced entry, no scratches or dents, and all my stuff was still in the car. So, what the hell had he been doing? Was it a case of trying to get into the wrong car by accident? But why did he run if that was true?

Could he have tampered with the brakes or something? Yes, I watch a lot of CSI. I was a tad unnerved by this recent development and I wasn't sure what I should do next. Call Nina? Call Zeb? The police maybe? I'd feel foolish having them come and look at a perfectly fine, unscathed car though. Wasn't Zeb supposed to be following me, anyway? Where was my Fairy Grim Reaper when I could use him? Oh yeah, probably getting cozy with Essie, I thought.

Damn it, I thought as I took my phone out and picked Zeb from the contacts. I was going to feel so dumb when he got here to look at basically nothing, but it felt wrong to just let this go without mentioning it to anyone. I didn't want to tell Nina because A) this amounted to nothing and B) after the first attempted mugging, if I reported this too, she might think I'm more trouble than I'm worth to have in her employment. And calling the police was overkill. The guy didn't take anything, didn't damage the car, and he didn't attack me. So Zeb it is.

"Walker," his smooth British accent came through the speaker. I sighed internally.

"Hey, Zeb. It's Cricket. Look, something weird happened just now—I mean, I'm ok, everything is ok, really. But it was strange, and I thought maybe I should tell you. I don't really want to call the cops or anything because... well, everything is fine. Can you just stop me from rambling now, please?" I bit my lip. Now that I said it out loud, it sounded even more pathetic.

Silence for a moment, then he said, "You're sure you're ok? Where are you?"

"I'm in the Starbucks parking lot," I said and gave him the address to the one I was at in downtown Nashville. "And yeah, I'm fine. You know what, this is stupid. You really don't need to come down here," I said and turned to look as I heard a motorcycle pulling into the parking lot behind me. I rolled my eyes and hung up the phone.

He parked in the spot next to Nina's car and took off his helmet. I glared. "Bluetooth," he said, pointing to his ears and taking out the ear buds.

"You've been following me again." I stated. I felt annoyed because if he was going to follow me, why wasn't he around when things actually happened? And—he's still following me. Both points were super irritating.

He smirked and got off the bike, walking to where I stood next to the car. "Right, but I'm keeping my distance. So what happened?" As I explained, he bent to inspect the car door, the handle, the window, and then he walked around and did the same to the other side. He kneeled and looked under the car. Then he popped the hood and had a look under there. I had no idea if he knew what he was doing, but it was making me feel better. But still annoyed.

"Anything gone from inside the car?" he asked, and I shook my head no. "Alright, did you get a look at him then?"

I wrinkled my nose. "Sort of, but not really. He was just a regular-looking guy wearing jeans, a white t-shirt, and a red hat. He got away before I could get close. What's your take? Just my dumb luck?" I asked.

He made a little grunting noise and said, "Princess, this could only happen to you." To which I flipped him the bird, and he smiled.

"Right. We don't know who the bloke was, what he wanted, why he didn't take anything, or where he went," Zeb summarized.

I smirked. "Exactly, Detective Walker. Thanks for the recap. Now what?" I asked.

"We wait for the next thing," he said, nonchalantly, returning to the bike and grabbing his helmet.

"We wait—what? What next thing?" I asked, confused.

"Princess, someone attempted to mug you recently. Now this. Maybe it was the same bloke, Chad, again. Maybe not, but either way, it's too much of a coincidence. If it's not the same bloke, then I think there's a common factor behind both events. Someone, somewhere, is after you," Zeb said.

I stared. Well, when you put it that way. "What do you think they want? And stop calling me Princess," I said.

He put the helmet on and smirked at me. "I don't know. But we'll get you prepared for next time. Follow me back to the house," Zeb said, getting on the bike.

"I have to finish delivering these packages for Nina first," I called over the roar of the bike's engine as he started it. There were only a few left, and the addresses were close by. I didn't want Nina upset that I didn't complete all the deliveries. Maybe they contained some time sensitive data.

Zeb motioned to his ears to show he couldn't hear me and then pointed to the road, meaning to follow him. I held up one finger, hoping to convey "give me a few minutes". He took off, and I got in the car and inspected my remaining envelopes. There were four. Huh, I could've sworn there were only three left. Okay, four more quick stops within about a ten-mile radius of Starbucks and I'd head home to see what Zeb meant by "preparing" me for the next time. I hoped to God there wouldn't be a next time.

About an hour later, I had delivered the remaining packages and was pulling into our shared driveway when I saw Zeb leaning against his bike. Had he been standing there for an hour? His expression was cross, and his face was red.

I shut the car off and almost as soon as I opened the door I heard, "Where the bloody hell have you been, Cricket?"

I paused and blinked a couple of times. Excuse me? So that's exactly what I said to him. "Excuse me?"

"You said you were following me straight home. You were attacked the other day and now someone has tried to break into your car. You've no bloody idea who it was or why and yet you're traipsing all over Nashville like you haven't a care in the world," he said, running his hand through his short blond hair. He pinned me with his gaze, which was still full of anger.

I gathered myself and walked over to stand right in front of him. I dropped my bag to the ground and poked him in the chest with my index finger. "You've got some nerve. So, you're supposed to be keeping me safe? That's your *job*? I am a grown ass woman and I've been looking out for myself for the past thirty-three years so I don't need you lecturing me about coming home a few minutes late when I was doing MY JOB." I punctuated those last two words with jabs to his chest. Zeb's mouth was hanging open in shock at this sudden turn of events.

"Cricket, I—" he began, and I cut him off.

"No, you listen to me. I don't know what's going on. You fed me this crazy story about who you are and why you're here and I was willing to believe it. You've moved in next door to me and I thought maybe there was a spark between us, you know? That kiss was incredible…" I trailed off, beginning to pace back and forth in front of our shared porch while Zeb looked on in confusion and disbelief.

"You thought it was incredible?" he said, the corners of his mouth turning up at that.

I ignored him and continued. "Then I met some gorgeous, exotic woman named Essie leaving your place late the other night. What's up with that? And what kind of name is 'Essie' anyway?" I said, returning to stand in front of him and poking him in the chest again. His broad, muscular chest, I might add.

"You met Essie? Cricket, let me explain," Zeb said, realization dawning. Then his mouth twitched as he tried not to laugh. "And what kind of name is 'Essie'? Bleeding hell, that's rich coming from a woman called Cricket," he said, trying to stifle a laugh.

I spun to face him, face rosy with anger and said, "It's a nickname for Christine!" I went to grab my bag off the ground so I could head inside and away from him. My face was burning with embarrassment and indignation. Before I could, he caught my wrists and pulled me up to meet his gaze.

"I quite like Christine. It's a beautiful name," he breathed, one side of his stupid, pouty mouth quirking up into a grin. "For a beautiful woman," he continued before his lips met mine. I pushed at his chest for just a moment. Then my treasonous arms were around his neck, my betraying hands in his hair, pulling him closer to me. His lips were so soft against mine and his arms went around my waist, pulling me to him. I kissed him with more intensity. A low growl escaped from Zeb's throat at that.

"Ahem."

We broke apart instantly at the sound. I turned to find my teenage daughter smirking at us from the porch. Clad in all black with her long black hair in pigtails, her perfectly smoked eyes rolled at us.

"God, Mom, am I the parent now? Should I ground you?" With a huff and a flick of her pigtail, she disappeared back inside the house. My daughter, Mac, the ultimate mood killer.

I turned back to Zeb, his lips pursed to contain his laughter. The moment I met his gaze, though, we both began laughing uncontrollably.

"So, I guess I should make sure she's not traumatized for life, huh?" Which brought forth a fresh wave of giggles from us both.

"Too right, we wouldn't want that," he said, the laughter subsiding. He grabbed my hand, bringing it to his lips and planting a gentle kiss on my knuckle.

"Goodnight, Princess," he said with a wink. "We'll talk more serious matters tomorrow, get some rest."

I nodded, smiling, "Goodnight… Sebby," I said and ran for my door.

"Sebby?" I heard, just as I closed the door behind me.

Chapter 12

The next day as I was out and about, I received a message from Carl at the Ministry of Vampire Affairs. I was being summoned to Sunshine Cleaners for a meeting with Carl and Nina. Oh boy, that sounded like a good time. Anyway, it wasn't until later this evening after they'd risen, so I'd have plenty of time to go home and get changed and maybe catch up with Zeb for a moment. We still had a few things to talk about from the night before. But before I headed home, I figured I'd swing by Forever Young and see Grandma. I would make her introduce me to Gus, once and for all.

I arrived at Forever Young, once again greeted by cat calls from the elderly men who hung out on the porch. I waved at them, gotta appreciate the effort and the ego boost, even if they were eighty-three and hadn't seen a woman without curlers in her hair for months. The girls at the front desk knew me by now, so I breezed past them after exchanging a friendly smile and kept an eye out for Grandma. She could be anywhere, social butterfly that she was.

I roamed up and down the halls and finally spotted Grandma coming out of Hot Yoga class. She was wearing a pink spandex leotard and a matching headband. She was wiping her face with a towel when she spotted me.

"Cricket! What a pleasant surprise. What brings you by dear?" Grandma broke away from the group of ladies she had been talking with and came over to hug me.

"Can't a girl just miss her grandma?" I said, squeezing her back. She smelled like lavender and Bengay.

Grandma chuckled. "Well certainly, but if I know my Cricket, that's not the only reason you're here," she said. "Oh! How are things going with Zeb?" she said, nudging my arm and waggling her eyebrows.

"A lady does not kiss and tell, Grandma," I said, taking her arm in mine as we walked down the hallway.

"Oh, so there's been some kissing, huh? That's my girl!" Grandma said, giggling like a schoolgirl.

I narrowed my eyes at her. "I did not come down here to dish on my love life or lack thereof, I came down here because A) I missed you and B) I demand to meet Gus. Now, Grandma," I said, sternly.

Grandma waved her free hand dismissively. "Oh Cricket, you worry too much. But let's see if he's around here somewhere. I wouldn't want to keep Princess Cricket waiting." She rolled her eyes at me and stepped up her pace, pulling me along with her.

"Have you been talking to Zeb, Grandma?" I said. I am not a Princess, damn it.

She ignored the question, which made me wonder if she had, in fact, spoken to Zeb recently but before I could ask, she was pulling me around a corner and we ran smack into a little old wrinkly man, hunched over and walking with a cane. He wore a tan fedora hat and tan slacks and a black Members Only jacket. He must be the only remaining member, I thought. When he looked up, I saw that he was wearing a pair of dark sunglasses.

"There you are, Sweets!" Grandma let go of my arm and transferred to this man's arm, who I now

110

assumed was the elusive Gus. I wondered why he was wearing sunglasses indoors as she turned to me, beaming. Gus's expression didn't change, but of course I couldn't see his eyes.

"Gus, this is Cricket! I've told you all about her, remember? She wanted to say hello!" Grandma turned to me, as if urging me to go ahead and say hello to Gus. I obliged.

"Hello," I said. I stuck my hand out to shake his, but after a few seconds I realized the gesture was being ignored, so I retracted, awkwardly. I felt a sudden wave of nausea as I put my hand down, but it was over quickly. Seriously, what did Grandma see in this man? So far, I was not impressed. I don't know what I expected, but he was not it.

"Cricket," he said, curtly. He turned to Grandma and said, "The boys are waiting for me to start the game, I've gotta run." He gave her a quick peck on the cheek, tipped his hat at me, and was off. Slowly, but he was off.

"Well, what do you think?" Grandma asked, looking after Gus with a cheeky grin on her face. Ewwww.

"I think he needs to learn some manners. Little rude, Grandma," I said, turning to look after him as well. He retreated slowly down the hallway toward whatever game awaited.

"Oh, he's just shy, Cricket," she said, swatting my arm.

I rolled my eyes. "What's with the sunglasses indoors?"

"He has a condition, sweetie," she said and then spotting one of her friends, dragged me into a

111

conversation that lasted about twenty minutes and covered everything from me, my divorce, my daughter, and Zeb, as if this woman cared about any of it.

I finally got away after looking at my watch and realizing that I needed to get home and change for the meeting with Carl and Nina later. I bid Grandma and her friend goodbye and headed out. The matter of Gus was not settled in my mind, however. I would be back to investigate further.

I went home to change clothes and attempt to cook dinner for my child before the meeting. But Mac called me from Luther's house where she informed me she could get a decent home cooked vegan meal. So, I freshened up and checked next door to see if Zeb was home, which he was not. I was eager to talk to him after my meltdown last night—followed by that amazing kiss—followed by Mac interrupting us before we could talk about anything. Like Essie. And the attempted... robbery? Car theft? Whatever it was, we needed to talk about it. We should really talk more about those kisses too, I thought.

I headed to Sunshine Cleaners after dusk and walked in to find Carl and Nina already waiting for me. I was getting nervous. Like, really nervous. Am I about to get fired? Drained of my blood? Turned into a vampire? Who knew? I really wished that I had followed up with Zeb on getting some vampire pepper spray right about now. Add that to the list of things that Zeb and I need to talk about, I noted.

I followed them into Carl's office after the perfunctory greetings and sat down on the pristine white sofa. Nina sat in a white chair opposite me and smiled sweetly. She never does that. What is going on? She was wearing a blood red suit and had her dark hair pulled back into a slick bun.

"Cricket, thanks for meeting us. Nina and I just wanted to make sure you're acclimating to your job duties. She also told me you happened up on a scheduled live feeding the other day and we wanted to make sure you didn't have any lingering questions about that," Carl said, clasping his hands together under his chin and glancing towards Nina. Carl wore a black suit and tie. He cut quite a striking image in the suit, paired with his pale skin and the shock of hair that kept spilling over his eyes.

"Yeah," I looked at my hands in my lap and back up at Nina. "I had hoped you hadn't realized I saw that," I said. I should have known. Damn vampire super hearing, I thought, how embarrassing.

"No problem, Cricket. I know it can be off-putting if you're new to the vampire lifestyle. But I don't want you to feel awkward or anxious at all. The woman you saw is a professional, she was not forced or coerced in any way," Nina said, her face a picture of geniality. She smiled then, and I wasn't sure what to do, so I smiled back.

"I'm fine. Very fine with it. No need to worry about me," I said, obviously not fine. Nina and Carl looked at one another, then back at me. I was beginning to have a very bad feeling about this.

"We have a proposition for you, actually. As you know, you've been performing basic, menial tasks for Nina and the reason for that is that we were making sure you could handle the vampire aspects of the job

113

before giving you anything else. You've done very well, even when you stumbled upon a feeding you shouldn't have seen, you handled it discreetly. That is a key characteristic of someone who will do well in the Ministry, Cricket. So, we have something more planned for you," Carl said. Nina was smiling and nodding beside him.

I frowned. "Something more?"

"We have many constituents in our society who have need of Daytime Concierge services. Until recently, we only provided Ministry authorities with these services. General vampire society members have been responsible for securing their own help with their personal and business matters. That is dangerous for them and for any humans they contract with," Carl said, leaning back in his chair, eyes still on me.

"We have decided it is in the best interest of our community, and the human community, to offer these services to our constituents through the Ministry. Considering this, we need someone responsible, respectable, and dignified to oversee this new department. We think you are that person, Cricket," Carl said, in his Russian accent, with a satisfied smile on his face. Nina looked about to burst with excitement, nodding her head and smiling from ear to ear.

Huh. I raised an eyebrow. They think I'm responsible, respectable, and dignified. Have they actually met me? I was still processing when Nina piped up.

"Of course, this new position would come with many more responsibilities. And a much larger paycheck," she said, smiling smugly. She knew the way to my heart was through my wallet, apparently.

I bit my lip. "How much more are we talking about?" I hated to be all about the cash, but damn it, I had a fifteen-year-old daughter whose heart was set on going to MIT.

Carl met my eyes with a satisfied smile. He knew they had me. He passed me an index card and when I turned it over and saw the number of zeros, I almost lost consciousness, but I kept my poker face on.

"What would my responsibilities be, exactly?" I asked, tucking the index card into my purse to drool over later.

"First, we would set you up with an office and an assistant. Then you would begin searching for candidates," Carl said.

"And how would I do that?" I asked. An office and an assistant... and I wouldn't have to take Fluffy to the groomer anymore? Sounded like heaven to me.

Carl smiled. "That will be entirely up to you, Cricket. Use whatever resources you have at your disposal and we will provide anything else you may need." Silence filled the room as I thought. Finally, Carl spoke again.

"Why don't you take the rest of the week off to think about things and wrap your head around it? You can start brainstorming ways to find DC candidates similar to the way Doreen found you. Also, maybe you'd like to have Doreen as your assistant? We can arrange that," he said with a glance at Nina, who smiled at me.

They wanted me to do this, and they wanted it badly. I could do with a week off to think.

"I'll take you up on that, Carl. I will need some time to think about all of this," I added, standing up and shouldering my bag.

Carl grinned, showing a little fang. "Of course. We'll be in touch later in the week," he said, rising from his chair to see me to the door. Nina stayed where she was. She seemed to be less enthusiastic than she had been earlier in our meeting.

I exited the building into the dark parking lot and found my car. I gripped the steering wheel and exhaled a huge breath I didn't realize I had been holding.

"Holy shit."

Chapter 13

After leaving Carl and Nina at Sunshine Cleaners, I headed back home. I was hoping to catch Zeb so we could talk about things. I pulled into the driveway to see his bike there—and the black Porsche. I huffed and wrinkled my nose. Essie. Frowning, I grabbed my bag and went into the house. Mac was lounging on the couch with a gigantic bowl of popcorn, watching "Property Brothers".

"Hey," she said, barely looking at me as she poked a couple pieces of popcorn into her mouth. She had her long black hair done up in a messy bun and was wearing black striped pajama pants with a white t-shirt that had a monster eating a cupcake on it. I sat down beside her on the couch and grabbed a handful of popcorn.

"You're home kind of early," I said. The lights were off in the living room and I could see Mac shrug in the dim light of the television.

"I just felt like coming home early tonight. Luther is being clingy. It's annoying," she said in between bites of popcorn.

I rolled my eyes at her. "That boy is a saint; you'll never convince me otherwise." She turned to give me a full-on smirk at that.

Just then, there was a knock at the door. I glanced at Mac and said, "Maybe Luther missed you." She stuck her tongue out at me as I moved to answer the door.

I opened it up to see Zeb standing there. He was wearing a black t-shirt, ripped jeans, and boots. He smiled and said, "Alright, Cricket? Hey, Mac."

117

I glanced back at Mac; she rolled her eyes and turned back to the television. I stepped out onto the porch with Zeb and pulled the door shut behind me.

"Hey," I said, smiling at him. There seemed to be a sudden shyness between us, like neither of us knew what to say or do now. I glanced out into the driveway and saw that the Porsche was gone. He followed my gaze and realized what I was looking for.

"I reckon I should explain about her. There's nothing going on between Essie and I. She's another Reaper, it's been all business, nothing more," he said. I felt the corner of my mouth quirk up into a slight smile at that.

"Oh. Well that's good to know," I said, biting my lip. I took a step closer to him.

He cleared his throat and glanced away. "And that bloke, Joey?"

I pursed my lips together to keep from smiling like a lunatic. "I think he likes me, but there's nothing going on there… on my end, anyway," I said.

"Well… that's good to know," he said back to me, his smile reaching his sparkling blue eyes. He took my hand and squeezed it once. He continued to hold on, his thumb stroking the back of my hand.

"I reckon we should sit down somewhere and talk about a couple things," he said, stepping closer to me.

I looked up at him. He was so close now. The surrounding air smelled like him, cedarwood and soap. I could reach up to touch the stubble of his beard if I wanted to. I could reach out and trace the tattoos on his bicep if I wanted to. I could stand on my tiptoes and kiss his sweet, pouty lips if I wanted to. Yeah, I definitely wanted to.

Before I could do any of that though, a chorus of "Don't Fear the Reaper" by Blue Oyster Cult blared from his cell phone and the spell was broken.

I laughed. "That's your ring tone?"

He grinned, letting go of my hand and pulling the phone from his back pocket. "Text alert." He was silent while he read, I could see all the levity drain from his expression.

"Something wrong?" I asked. I was still reeling from our little moment just now, but I could tell that whatever the text contained, it was not good news.

"It's Edward Lambert. He's dead." Zeb put the phone down and looked at me, worry creasing his brows.

"Oh my God! What? Wait, who texted you about it?" I said, my hand flying to my mouth in shock. Edward, Nina's human husband, was dead. Was it his failing health or had something else happened? I remembered his plea to me that day I had met him at Nina's house.

"Work. Duty calls, Princess," Zeb said. Oh yeah... the Reaper thing.

"So, you have to like, collect his soul or something now?" I said, honestly curious. We had never talked about any of this and I genuinely wondered what his job entailed.

He smirked. "Something like that," he said. "Go get some rest tonight, we'll talk tomorrow. Obviously, this opens up a whole new can of worms we'll need to sort out." He ran his hand through his spiky blond hair, blowing out an exasperated breath.

119

"No, I'm coming with you. I need to see Nina, make sure she's okay. Let me get my bag," I said, moving towards my door.

"Cricket, it's not safe. I never know what I'll find when I get to—the job site," he said, hesitating over that last part. "Besides, with you working for Nina and the stuff that's been going on recently, we don't know if any of it is related to Edward's death. I'd feel better if you just stayed here, where I know you'll be relatively safe," Zeb said.

"That's exactly why I need to go. What if it is related? I need to find out what happened and try to piece things together. And at the very least, maybe I can be there for Nina if she needs anything," I said, determined that he would not leave me behind. He might as well find out now, I'm not the kind of girl who stays behind.

Zeb sighed and pinched the bridge of his nose. He was silent for a moment, probably debating whether it was worth a fight. He closed his eyes briefly, then opened them and said, "Right, if nothing else will do you, then let's go. But what I say goes. It's my job and I call the shots, agreed?" He raised an eyebrow and waited for my response.

"Agreed," I said sweetly, crossing my fingers behind my back. How adorable he was, he had no idea who he was dealing with, did he?

Inside, I found Mac asleep on the couch, the television still on. I tucked a blanket around her, turned the tv off, and grabbed my bag. I went outside to find Zeb starting the Harley and adjusting his helmet. He tossed a second helmet to me, which I caught clumsily. I quickly put it on and climbed onto the back of the bike, wrapping my arms around Zeb's waist. I could definitely get used to this, I thought.

We arrived at Nina's house amid a flurry of activity. It seemed everyone in Davidson county had rushed right over as soon as word got out about Edward's death. There were even news reporters out front trying to get the scoop. Zeb flashed an ID at a few people and before I knew it, we were standing in Nina's living room. She was under a blanket on the couch, crying, while another woman sat beside Nina, consoling her.

Nina noticed us enter the room, and she stood to meet us. "Mr. Walker, I was expecting you. Cricket," she tilted her head with a confused expression. "How do you know Mr. Walker?"

"He's my... neighbor," I said, sneaking a look at Zeb. His lips twitched with the effort of concealing a smile.

Nina still looked baffled. Who accompanies their Grim Reaper neighbor on house calls? Right, that would be me. "Oh, I see," she said, clearly not seeing.

"I'm so sorry, Nina," I continued, ignoring her confusion. "What can I do?" I asked her.

"Thank you, dear. To be honest, I'm not sure yet." She sank back down onto the couch with that.

"What exactly happened, Nina? Anything amiss?" Zeb asked, looking around the room.

Nina dabbed at her eyes with a Kleenex. "I don't think so. It must have just been his time, he'd been sick for so long, you know," she said. The woman next to her patted Nina's arm.

121

"Can we see him?" Zeb asked. I looked at him, horrified. See him? Oh right, he probably needs to see him. I wasn't sure I wanted to though.

Nina sobbed at that. She nodded, dabbing her eyes again. "Yes, upstairs." She nodded to the stairway on our right.

Zeb looked at me and nodded his head toward the stairs, indicating I should follow him. So I did. I had never been to the second floor of Nina's house before, so I let Zeb lead the way. Not that he probably knew where he was going either, but I'd let him worry about that.

"So," I said as we trudged up step after step. "Nina said she was expecting you. She knows who you are?" I asked as we reached the landing.

Zeb turned to look at me. "Yes, vampires know about us. Humans do too, but they like to pretend we're not real," he said, surveying the second floor and motioning for me to follow.

"What are you gonna do? You didn't bring your scythe," I said, and when he turned to give me an incredulous look, I winked and smiled at him.

Finally, we found ourselves in front of a door that was partially open. A couple of nurses came out just as we were about to go in. Edward's body laid on the massive king-sized bed, looking tiny and shriveled in comparison. His skin was even paler than I'd remembered and looked almost translucent. The white tufts of hair still stood out in every direction on his head. But he wasn't in there anymore, he was gone. I'd hardly known him and yet, it made me feel sad.

Zeb approached the body. He took out his phone and began looking back and forth from the body to the screen, tapping buttons. He noticed me checking out his phone and said, "Everything is just information, Princess, even souls. All ones and zeros." He grinned and continued whatever he was doing. Who knew Reapers were so technologically advanced? I guess there really was an app for everything, I thought.

After a few minutes, I started looking around the room because honestly, I was getting bored with his iPhone soul collecting process. The room was tidy, blankets folded up lying here and there, medicine bottles and books on the nightstand. I picked up the book on top of the stack, "Living with a Vampire: A Guide to Coping and Cohabitating". As I lifted it, a scrap of paper fell out onto the floor. I bent down to pick it up, flipped it over and saw an address on it. My jaw dropped.

Zeb was still working, walking back and forth around the bed, tapping on his phone. He caught sight of me, saw my expression, and stopped what he was doing. "What's wrong, Cricket?"

"This slip of paper fell out of this book," I said, holding it up for him to see. He took it, looked at the address and back to me, confused.

"So?" he asked, handing it back to me.

"I delivered a package to this address yesterday, after the 'almost car theft' or whatever it was," I whispered. Now his mouth was hanging open. He recovered quickly, though. He held a finger up to his mouth to indicate that I should shut the hell up. He glanced back at the door to make sure there was no one around.

"We'll discuss it later, don't say anything else," he whispered. Then, he quickly pulled up the camera app on his phone and snapped a photo of the address. He put it back inside the book and replaced the book on the nightstand. Then he went back to work.

My mind was reeling, however. Did that address and the inhabitant have something to do with Edward's death? Was it more than just natural causes then? Was it my fault somehow? I wished Zeb would hurry so we could discuss it. I paced the room until finally he stood in my path.

"I'm done," he said. He held out his arm, the one with the tattoos of the beautiful flora and fauna surrounding the scythe. He pointed to an area on his forearm and as I watched, a tiny line of ink disappeared.

"What the—Did you see that? How did that happen?" I said, instinctively reaching out a finger to touch the spot where the ink had been. Tattoos don't just vanish. Many people probably wished they would, I thought.

I looked at Zeb to see a wistful smile playing on his lips as he stared at the spot, then looked at me. "I'll explain later, I just wanted you to see it," he said. "We have more important things to discuss now. First, we need to get out of here," he said, heading for the door.

I glanced back at Edward's lifeless body on the bed. He didn't look any different now that Zeb had collected his soul. I wondered what happened to souls, and if any of the things I thought I knew about life after death was true now that I was aware of vampires, reapers, and other things that go bump in the night.

Forever intertwined in the supernatural world now, I had a sudden stab of fear in my chest. I realized once and for all that all of this was very real. And if the address turned out to be linked to Edward's death and to my delivery there, I was in a lot of trouble. I backed away from the bed and out the door, following Zeb down the stairs.

Chapter 14

It was very late. Or early, depending on how you looked at it. Zeb and I found ourselves at Waffle House at two in the morning, having breakfast. I was having waffles, and he was having a loaded omelet. Zeb had finished eating and was busy looking up the address from the scrap of paper on his phone. I pushed the last couple of bites of waffle around on my plate, my appetite vanishing.

"Bloody hell," he said, tossing the phone down on the table. Another patron glanced over at us and scowled.

"Progress?" I asked, taking a small bite of my waffles.

He ran one hand through his spiky blond hair and sighed. "Chadwick Morrow is the occupant at 652 Crestmoor Road. Also known as Mugger Chad," he said.

"Wait, my Mugger Chad?" I said, pausing mid-chew.

"No, Cricket. The other Mugger Chad," he said, exasperated. He pinched the bridge of his nose and closed his eyes for a moment. "Which means all of this is most definitely connected and you are most definitely involved. Damn," he said.

I pursed my lips, thinking. This is not good. "So, what do we do now?"

"*We* don't do anything… *I* will track this bloke down and find out what the bloody hell is going on," Zeb said.

I huffed. "Think again," I said, raising an eyebrow.

"Cricket, no. We have no idea what is going on. Someone may have killed Edward; they've already attacked you. I can't risk it," Zeb said, shaking his head no. What did he mean *he* couldn't risk it? Did he mean personally or professionally that he couldn't risk me getting hurt? I made a mental note to revisit that later.

He rose from the booth, throwing some money down to cover the bill and a hefty tip as we left. I was fuming, so I stayed silent. I quietly put my helmet on and got on the bike behind Zeb, wrapping my arms around him. I wasn't enjoying it as much as I normally would've, damn it. I couldn't believe he wanted me to stay out of this when I was so clearly involved already. It wasn't possible. Telling me to stay home while he went out to take care of everything was like asking the sun not to shine. And if that's the kind of relationship he wanted, he had found the wrong girl.

We rode in complete silence all the way back to the house. After we pulled into the drive, I hopped off the bike and pulled the helmet off immediately. I had turned to stomp up the porch stairs when he caught my arm.

"Alright, Princess? What's wrong?"

I spun around. "What's wrong? Zeb, you can't expect me to just sit at home and knit a sweater while you go out and put yourself in danger. This already involves me, very much so. I need to help unravel this. You need me to help, you just won't admit it," I said, hands on hips, scowling at him.

Now it was his turn to scowl. "I bloody well can expect you to stay out of it. It's my job to keep you safe and I intend to do that," he said, getting off the bike and facing me, also with hands on hips. He looked hot when he scowled, I thought. Focus, Cricket.

"You can tell your employers not to worry about me. Why the hell do they care if I live or die, anyway? So, if all I am is a job responsibility, consider yourself relieved of duty." I slung the helmet at him, which he caught as it knocked him back a couple of steps.

"Cricket! You know that's—" he started.

I slammed the door behind me, cutting him off. It was seriously late, or early now. Good thing Carl had given me the rest of the week to think and gear up for my new job responsibilities. The couch was empty, so Mac had woken and gone to her bed at some point. I paused in the middle of the living room and ran my hands through my long hair. Exhausted, I stomped up the stairs and threw myself into bed. I'd lie there and fume at Zeb for a while, and hopefully I'd fall asleep at some point.

A couple hours later, and my plan wasn't working. I had gone to bed, tossed and turned, yelled at Zeb some more in my head, and finally I gave up. I went downstairs and made a pot of coffee. Mac was gone. Her huge black backpack was missing from the foyer. I peeked outside; Zeb's bike was missing also. So, I puttered around the house for a few hours, doing chores, drinking coffee, and scrolling Facebook. I finally decided I should take myself out shopping.

I hadn't gone shopping since I started my new job. I was making three times what I made as a paralegal, I could afford to treat myself. And Mac. I showered, put on my favorite jeans and a pink crop top.

I attempted to do my makeup, like in the tutorial Mac made me watch on YouTube, only it never quite looked right when I did it. I studied my reflection in the mirror and decided I was presentable. I scraped my hair up into a cute messy bun and grabbed my bag.

By the time I left home, it was mid-afternoon. I was headed towards the mall when I noticed the street sign for Crestmoor Road as I drove past. Huh. That was the address from the slip of paper, where Mugger Chad was living. Maybe I should drive by and check it out? Zeb would not approve, Logical Cricket thought. So Irrational Cricket immediately did a U-turn and turned onto Crestmoor. I thought I remembered the house number was 652, so I cruised along at a moderate speed, looking for the number. I turned down the Rolling Stones I had been blasting on the radio so I could concentrate. *I can't get no satisfaction either, Mick.* I slowed the car to a crawl… 648, 650, there it was, 652.

What appeared to be Nina's black SUV was in the driveway. I couldn't be sure at first, because didn't all black SUVs look the same? But I finally saw the Sunshine Cleaners sticker on the back window and confirmed; it was Nina's vehicle. What the hell? How did she know Mugger Chad? What was going on?

I drove past at a snail's pace, trying to see what I could. Which was nothing. There was another car there, a gray Nissan Altima, but I could see no activity. I grabbed my huge black sunglasses from the console, the ones that look like insect eyes. I put them on and drove on past. I circled back around, making a large loop that took about ten minutes for me to complete, and returned to Chad's house. Nothing had changed, so

I parked a few blocks away on the opposite side of the street to do some surveillance.

About five minutes into my impromptu surveillance of the house, I got bored. I would make a terrible cop, I decided, taking my phone out and checking Facebook. Cute dogs, political rants, and pictures of my Aunt Rose's latest quilt made up the content of my news feed. Boring. How do detectives work like this? I thought. Still nothing at the house. I sighed. Maybe I should just go to the mall as I had originally intended and give this up. I probably should call Zeb and apologize for getting so upset, even though I was right, I thought. Still, I shouldn't have stormed off and slammed the door in the middle of our argument.

I took out my phone again and dialed Zeb. Just as I pushed the button to call him, I noticed the door of the house opening and out came Chad. I quickly pushed the end button so I could pay attention to what was happening.

Chad emerged, wearing jeans and a red t-shirt. His brown hair was a mass of unruly curls and he wore glasses. He was carrying a suitcase which he put into Nina's SUV. He looked around as he did, making me instinctively duck down. Not suspicious behavior at all, Cricket. He then returned to the house and closed the door behind him.

What was Nina doing here during the day anyway, I thought. She should be at home, in her light tight coffin or whatever it was that modern-day vampires slept in. I'd heard that some vampires could rise earlier and stay up later, but staying up all day was out of the question as far as I knew, no matter their age. It didn't take a professional detective to know something was going on here. And I was excited that I had discovered it, all by myself. Who needed a flipping Grim Reaper's help, anyway? I sure didn't.

So, what do I do now? I wondered, after my excitement waned, and boredom set in again. Should I see if Nina's SUV was open and try to find out what was in the suitcase? Should I stay put and just watch for her to come out? Should I knock on the door and say I'm selling Avon?

Just then, I got a text from Doreen saying Carl had filled her in about our new jobs. She sounded excited. I texted back and said we should meet up tomorrow to talk about it. Then I waited some more. I played a few rounds of Candy Crush on my phone and still, there was no activity at the house. I browsed Amazon and purchased a cute purse and some shoes to match. I scanned the local news website. Still, nothing.

With a sigh, I decided I could catch a quick nap since Chad and Nina weren't doing much of anything, so I set the alarm on my phone to wake me in one hour and I reclined the seat, closing my eyes. By then, it would be dusk, and if Nina was coming out, it would happen then.

Chapter 15

I woke to the sound of someone tapping on the window of my car. Disoriented at first, I noticed it was dark out, but after a few moments I remembered where I was and why just as I saw Mugger Chad at my car window. Busted. He had a grim expression on his face as he tapped on the window again. It was then I noticed the pistol in his other hand.

Tempted to turn the ignition key as quickly as I could and speed out of there, I knew it was likely he could shoot me quicker than I could escape. So, I rolled the window down and smiled as sweetly as I could with what felt like a lead ball in my stomach.

Before I could speak, he said, "Get out. Don't make a scene, I'll shoot." Silently, I grabbed my bag and opened the car door. He motioned for me to follow him, so I did, and he swiftly took my keys and shoved them into his jacket pocket.

I tried not to panic, but I seemed to be failing miserably at that. He's got a gun and now he's got me inside the house and away from my car. Think, Cricket, I told myself. All I could come up with was that I should talk and get him talking as well. All my years of watching CSI had better pay off, I thought.

"Nice place," I attempted, looking around at the house after we were inside. It wasn't bad as far as that goes. The living room was neat and comfy looking with a large couch, coffee table, and lots of books and magazines. It looked kind of cozy.

"Shut up," Chad said, poking me in the ribs with the gun. He inched me forward until I was in front of the sofa, so I sat down. He noticed me looking at him and said, "Yeah, I'm the guy who mugged you."

Before I could control myself, I said, "Almost mugged me." His face darkened at that, and I knew it had been a mistake. Focus, Cricket. Keep him talking. "So why did you do that, anyway?"

He ignored me. This is going great, I thought to myself. Silently, he took my bag and slung it onto the countertop in the kitchen and turned to face me.

"Why have you been sitting in your car out there all day?" he asked. My face went red. Damn, I thought I was being so slick, and he had known I was out there the whole time. Wait… he knew I was out there the whole time?

"If you knew I was out there, why didn't you come and get me sooner? Do you realize how boring a stakeout is when you're alone?" I blurted.

Out of the corner of my eye, I saw Nina stride into the room. "Cricket, I'm so disappointed in you. I had thought you were the perfect employee," she said, looking fabulous as always. She sat down regally in the chair opposite from me and crossed her legs. Chad just about fell over himself bringing her a glass of wine.

"What the hell is going on, Nina?" I asked. At that, Chad hurried over to me and poked me in the neck with the gun.

"Shut up!" he yelled.

Nina waved a hand in the air dismissively, "That's not necessary, Chad." He put the gun down and stalked away. She turned her attention to me. After a few moments of silently appraising me and swirling the wine in her glass, she spoke.

"I agreed to hire you to be my Daytime Concierge for one reason only. I knew my husband was dying and eager to speed up the process, which normally wouldn't have been a problem for me. But as I'm sure you've heard by now, he hired a witch to curse his son, Aaron, and I if he died before reaching age seventy-three," she said and waved her hand once again.

"It should have been water under the bridge years ago, but he held on to his anger at me for turning Aaron. So he had an old warlock cast that spell. He's enjoyed having that hanging over my head for years now. It prevented me from turning Edward or having him killed, not that I would've done such a thing. Honestly, his lack of trust in me was insulting," she said, leaning back in the chair and taking a sip of the wine.

I sat silently, listening. I knew some of this from Doreen already, but I was finally getting the whole story. Maybe this would explain everything, if I could make it out of here without Chad shooting me or poking me to death with the damn gun. Keep it together, Cricket, keep her talking.

"So, what was the curse? And why would he curse you for turning Aaron? Didn't Aaron ask you to turn him into a vampire?" I asked, gripping the arm of the sofa and trying to keep cool.

Nina barked a curt laugh. "Of course, Aaron wanted it. I wouldn't have turned him otherwise. He was in love with me, he wanted to be with me forever after his father died." At my unwitting expression of disgust, she looked affronted. "When you have eternal life, you look at things much differently, dear." She took another drink of the wine, holding the glass in front of her and swirling it around.

"The curse stated that if Edward died before age seventy-three, that Aaron and I would become mortal. Human, once again," she said, her words dripping with contempt. "He felt it was a measure of protection, that Aaron and I wouldn't be able to kill him off to be together and inherit all of his money," she sighed.

"And why seventy-three? I really don't know. His father died at that age, so maybe he just thought that was a good age to go." She smirked and swirled the wine around in her glass, glancing up at me. "And he did it. He died at age seventy-two, fifty-one weeks, three days," she added, taking a larger drink. Chad came back to refill her glass. I was thinking I could use a glass myself right about now, but I kept quiet.

Nina turned her attention back to me. "And that's where you come into play, dear Cricket," she said, staring at me.

"Me? What do I have to do with any of this?" I asked, stunned. So far it sounded like Edward and Nina had had a nightmare of a marriage. How was that my fault?

Nina scowled and glanced at Chad, who hung his head in shame. "Ah, that brings me back to one of the reasons I hired you in the first place. I knew that Edward would attempt to speed his death somehow, to punish us. I didn't know what he would do or how he would do it, but I knew that if I hired you, a young and beautiful human, that Edward wouldn't be able to resist speaking to you. I knew he would ask for your help. And I know that he did in fact do so, some days ago," she continued, examining her red fingernails while holding her wine glass.

I flashed back to the day that Edward had tottered into the Lambert's living room and attempted to secure my help in hastening his own death. "I didn't say I'd help him, in fact I told him that helping him with anything at all was not in my job description," I said, sitting up straighter on the couch and my voice growing louder.

Nina smiled. "Shhhhh. Shhhhh, sweet Cricket. I know. I know you didn't purposefully help him, which is why you're still breathing." I gulped.

"But the fact remains that you did help him," she said. She stopped swirling her drink and examining her nails and looked directly at me with those beautiful whiskey-colored eyes.

"You failed to tell me about the car being broken into," she said. Her gaze was immobilizing; I couldn't look away. I felt like I couldn't even breathe while she looked at me so intently.

"Someone placed a package in the car, which you delivered. I believe you delivered this package to someone who helped Edward end his life, which activated the curse on Aaron and me. I need you to tell me where you delivered the package," she said, turning her gaze on Chad once again. "*He* was supposed to be monitoring you and your activities, but somehow he was otherwise occupied that day," she said, her voice dripping with anger.

Chad recoiled. "I told you, I saw her go into Starbucks. She was in there a really long time and I fell asleep. I'm sorry, Nina," he said, imploring her.

I had been absorbing all of this information when I remembered the first time I had met Chad. "Wait. You had Chad following me just to watch what I was doing? Why the hell did he try to mug me, then?" I said, staring daggers at Chad. He looked sheepish at that.

Nina turned her icy gaze on Chad once again. "You mugged her? I did not tell you to mug her," Nina spat. She slammed her wine glass down on the table beside her.

Chad's face turned red. "I didn't actually mug her. Her boyfriend caught me and beat me up pretty bad. Then they called the cops," He looked at me with disdain while touching his nose gingerly. He turned his attention back to Nina. "You hadn't paid me yet, and I needed some cash," he said, shrugging.

Nina rolled her eyes and turned back to me. "Cricket, I apologize for that inconvenience. I did not hire Chad to mug you. I had no idea I hired such a bumbling idiot," she said, glaring at him.

I stared, incredulously. Inconvenience? I started to argue but thought better of it. I'll circle back around to this when I don't have a bumbling idiot pointing a gun in my direction every five minutes, I thought.

"Let's get back to the problem at hand, shall we? I need the addresses you delivered to that day, Cricket," Nina said, leveling her gaze at me.

I sighed. "Do you think I have a photographic memory? I picked up a package, plugged the address into the GPS, and followed the directions it gave me to get there," I said, with a shrug. Then it hit me. The GPS! "Did you check the GPS in the car?" I said, looking from Nina to Chad.

Nina looked at Chad to confirm. Realization dawned on him, as evidenced by his expression. "You didn't check the GPS, did you? Why in hell did I hire you?" Nina spat, throwing her hands in the air.

He stammered, "I didn't think—" but Nina cut him off.

"You didn't think, that's precisely the problem," Nina growled, then turned to me. "Come, Cricket, show me the GPS and the address history," she said, rising from the chair and giving Chad a last look of disgust.

"You—stay here until I give you further instructions," she spat in his direction.

I smiled smugly at Chad while following Nina to the front door. He frowned at me. I moved faster to keep up with Nina because he was still holding the gun, after all.

Chapter 16

Nina drove us back to her place in her SUV, leaving my car on the street near Chad's place, which I wasn't happy about. However, I took comfort in the fact that I had thought to grab my purse off the counter before we left so Chad couldn't rifle through it. Nina was silent most of the way to her house, I could tell she was angry and stressed out. I was wondering about the curse and how it was affecting her, or would affect her, but I said nothing. I didn't want to upset her further and risk my safety in the process.

When we arrived, she opened the garage door, and we both went straight to the SUV I used when I was running her errands. Which I would not be doing anymore, I thought gleefully, but kept a straight face. I reached in and removed the GPS from the dash and turned it on. The history was still there, and I tossed it to Nina.

"There it is, that's everywhere I've been while driving your car." She caught it awkwardly and looked at it with a puzzled expression, then back to me.

"Which one should we visit first?" she asked, looking at the device and turning it over in her hands as if it was some sort of alien technology. To her, it probably was.

"*We* aren't visiting any of them. *I* am going home and you can do whatever the hell you want," I said, turning to go. Where to, I had no idea, since I didn't have my car and it was fully dark out now.

I supposed I could walk a few blocks and then call Zeb or Doreen to come get me. Tired, frustrated, and embarrassed, I couldn't care less about how Nina received my words. I didn't think Carl would fire me. Besides, I had a lot of dirt on Nina now too, so I felt much less threatened by her and anything she could do to me.

Then, Nina surprised me by pulling her own tiny, pearl-handled pistol out of her purse. She smiled. "You were saying?"

I blew out a breath. This day just keeps getting better. Why hadn't I just gone to the damn mall? Why hadn't I ever let Zeb give me that vampire mace thingy for my key chain? "I believe I was saying, we should start with the first address on the list," I said, glaring as I stomped back to the SUV, with Nina and the GPS in tow.

After hitting several of the addresses from the GPS and having no luck, we arrived on Caldwell Avenue in front of a large two-story Colonial house. I vaguely remembered being here and dropping off an envelope a couple days before. Nothing special stuck out in my memory about it though.

Nina studied the exterior of the house and then said, "Come."

We exited the vehicle, and I followed her to the front porch. She rang the bell, and we waited. And waited some more. She banged on the storm door, and we waited again. Finally, a young black woman who looked as if she could be friends with my daughter answered the door. She had shoulder length, wavy, black hair, black lipstick, and wore a black formal gown. She looked back and forth from Nina and I, frowning.

"Who are you?" she said in a Jersey accent, with a smidgen of disdain. She snarled her lip. I peered behind her into the house and could see many candles burning, and I could smell incense burning as well. I was thinking we'd found the right house at this point, especially when I felt goosebumps prickle on my arms and a general feeling of uneasiness started to envelope me.

Apparently, Nina thought we had the right house too because her arm shot out to grab the door before the girl could close it on us.

Nina smiled insidiously and said, "We would like a word," in a low, growling voice, her fangs lowered just a bit. She forced her way inside with me on her heels.

The girl's demeanor changed instantly, and her eyes glowed red. I shoved the "holy shit" thoughts I was having to the back of my brain for later contemplation and instantly decided I'd call the witchy girl Bellatrix for simplicity's sake, being a Harry Potter fan and all.

Bellatrix began reciting some words that sounded like Greek or maybe Latin. Sparks flew from her fingertips, but Nina was faster. With her vampire speed she grabbed Bellatrix in a headlock and with fangs fully bared, Nina said, "Be a good girl and tell us where your mommy is before I make a midnight snack out of you," her fangs poised above the girl's neck where I could see a large vein throbbing.

"Robbie! Robbie!" The girl's strangled call for help from Robbie, whoever the hell he was, escaped her lips as she grappled with Nina. I watched, unsure what I could or even should do.

I watched the two of them struggle amid flying sparks and I saw a man, presumably Robbie, running from the back of the house towards us. As I watched him approach and wondered what I should do, I felt a hand on my shoulder. Almost instantly, large, muscular arms wrapped around me and pulled me out of the house and into the nearby bushes. I tried to scream, but a hand was over my mouth faster than I could make a sound. I struggled against their hold when they spun me around and I saw it was Zeb.

I couldn't begin to explain how grateful I was to see him and how humiliated I felt after the day I'd had and how our last encounter had ended. But all that mattered now was that he was here, and we could get the hell out of here and away from whatever supernatural smack down was about to happen in that house.

Zeb held a finger up to his mouth, indicating I should shut up and motioned for me to follow him. He held my hand as we ran through the neighboring yards, jumping over flower beds, tearing through bushes, and weaving our way in and out of various lawn furniture and fences. By the time we reached his Harley, I was breathing hard and had a stitch in my side. I should go to the gym more often, I thought, trying to catch my breath before Zeb noticed.

He quickly got on the bike and pulled me onto it behind him, forgoing our helmets to get out of there as fast as possible. He revved the engine, and we sped away, while I hung on to Zeb tightly.

Chapter 17

Back at the house, Zeb and I sat at the dining room table drinking coffee, eating doughnuts, and discussing the day's events. It was late. Mac was upstairs, asleep in her room. Shaken and exhausted, I sighed and leaned back against the chair.

"How did you know where to find me? Was it your Grim Reaper spidey senses?" I asked, sipping my coffee. Zeb sat across the table from me, nursing his own mug of coffee.

He rolled his eyes. "After you slammed the door in my face last night, I came looking for you so I could apologize. You were nowhere to be found, even Mac hadn't seen you. That's not like you, so I got in touch with Doreen. She said you'd texted her earlier in the day, so I tracked it," he said nonchalantly as he took a bite of a doughnut.

"Wait, you can track a text? I didn't know that was a thing. Also, you can just go around tracking texts whenever you want to?" I asked with mock exasperation.

He smiled and raised an eyebrow. "Perk of the job," he said, taking a drink of his coffee. "Anyway, I found your car parked near the address we found in Edward's book. I had someone bring it back here, by the way. And after I asked you not to go there on your own, but we'll circle back to that." I rolled my eyes at him.

"By that time, you and Nina had gone, which I found out from Chad." At that, Zeb looked at the knuckles on his right hand and stretched his fingers out.

145

"Please tell me you punched that douchebag," I said. Chad was such a jerk and one tiny part of me felt a little sorry for him and the fact that he would have to face Nina's wrath. But a much larger part of me was dying to hear that Zeb had roughed him up a little, and in my honor too. Swoon.

The corner of Zeb's mouth turned up as he tried to suppress a smile. "His nose will never be the same, let's just leave it at that," he said, winking at me. "I found out he'd been holding you at gunpoint all day and I couldn't help myself. Bloody tosser had it coming to him," he said.

I had to admit, that was kinda hot. But I would not admit it to Zeb.

"The wanker finally told me you and Nina were using the GPS to trace your deliveries. So I called in a favor at work, got the addresses, and arrived just in time to find you and Nina in the middle of getting your arses handed to you by a coven of witches. So, I grabbed you and got us the hell out of there," Zeb said, placing his empty mug on the table.

I sighed. "All in a day's work for a Reaper, I suppose. Speaking of Nina, she filled me in while I was her guest," I said, with a smirk.

I gave Zeb a recap on the curse and everything I'd learned from Nina about her relationships with Edward and Aaron. I told him why Chad had tried to mug me, too. Judging by Zeb's facial expression, I feared that he would pay Chad another visit sometime soon.

After listening intently, Zeb leaned back in his chair and rubbed his beard, deep in thought. "So, this house on Caldwell. You're sure that's where you delivered the package, the one that Edward had someone place in your car?"

"Judging by that chick's reaction when Nina and I knocked on her door, I'm sure. But that's all I know, unfortunately," I said, sipping my now lukewarm coffee. I wondered how Nina had fared after Zeb had swept me away from the house. Surely, she got away. Why did I even care though, after today?

Zeb was quiet for a few moments, then he said, "I'm going back there then." And after seeing the indignant expression on my face, he corrected himself. "I mean, *we* are going back there," he looked at me and I grinned. I would save the victory dance for later.

"Nina still has it out for me since I delivered the package. She knows it wasn't intentional, but I think she still needs someone to blame. Also, she'll still be looking for a way to lift the curse," I said, mostly just thinking out loud.

I glanced at the clock and saw that it was nearly six am. We'd been up all night. Mac should've been up and making some sort of vegan concoction for breakfast by now.

"I'll be right back, I'm gonna wake Mac up for school," I said to Zeb, rising from my seat and letting my hand graze his back as I passed by. Did I detect a slight shiver at that? I smiled to myself as I ascended the stairs.

I opened the door to Mac's room, which was completely dark. Not only were the lights off, but she'd drawn the black curtains as well. I flipped the switch and said, "Rise and shine, sweet cheeks," only to discover her bed was empty. The bed looked slept in, but she was gone now.

I pushed the panic down that was rising inside of me and looked around the room. Everything looked as it should, except the fact that her giant black backpack was still here. She never went anywhere without that thing. It held her iPad, her journals, her drawing pad, makeup, basically everything a teenage girl needs to survive in the world. Without it, she wouldn't know what to do with herself. So why the hell was it still sitting in her room and she wasn't here?

I raced to the bathroom and slung the shower curtain back. No Mac. I ran to my room and flipped on the light. No Mac. Now I was panicking.

"Mac! MAC!" I called as I ran from room to room, hoping and praying to find her rolling her perfectly smoked eyes at me and flipping her black hair, saying "God, Mom, you're so annoying." But after checking every room, I realized she was not in the house.

Zeb came running after me as soon as he heard me calling for her. "She's gone?" he asked, following me as I went from room to room a second time, flipping on lights, pulling back covers, and opening closet doors. I didn't answer, I was too busy trying to think. Could she be at Luther's house? She loved Luther's house; his mother fed her.

I raced to the kitchen to find my bag with my phone inside, Zeb on my heels. I dug out my phone and with shaking hands, I found Luther in the contacts. I'd made Mac program his number into my phone months ago, just in case I ever needed it. And now, I needed it.

Zeb stood close as I waited for Luther to pick up. I pushed the speaker button so he could hear as well. It rang several times, and I was ready to scream

148

by the time I heard Luther's groggy voice say, "Hello? Mrs. Jones?"

"Yes, Luther. Hey, is Mac at your house by any chance? Did she stay over or something? You're not in trouble if she did, I just need to find her," I said, the words coming out in a rush. I ran my free hand through my long blonde hair and paced the kitchen while Zeb leaned against a counter, listening intently.

Silence followed for a few beats. "Luther! Are you listening to me? Where is Mac?" I said with impatience. Zeb grabbed my free hand as I paced and stopped me in front of him. I gave him a worried look, and he squeezed my hand.

"I haven't seen her since she left last night, Mrs. Jones. I swear, she left and said she was going home. Didn't she come home last night?" he asked, sleep still evident in his voice. Well now I was feeling like Parent of the Year because if Mac was indeed missing, I had no idea what time she had come home and what time she had disappeared because I was out participating in a supernatural melee. I closed my eyes and sighed, pinching my nose with my free hand.

"I think she did, her bed looks slept in but she's not here now. Her backpack is still here, though. I'm worried. Did she mention any early morning plans or anything?" I asked Luther, my voice small and weary.

Luther cleared his voice on the other end of the line. "No, ma'am, she didn't. I was gonna pick her up for school this morning, like always." I could sense worry in his voice now, too. I glanced at Zeb, standing next to me, hands on hips. He looked as if he were deep in thought. My call waiting beeped as Luther was in mid-sentence.

149

"Someone's beeping in, maybe it's her! I'll call you later, Luther!" I said, hanging up on him as I switched the line to answer the incoming call. "Mac?" I said, forgoing the niceties at this point.

"Mom? *Mom*?" I heard Mac's panicked voice on the other end of the line, then another familiar voice began speaking.

"Cricket, so nice to know you made it home safely after our little squabble with the witches," Nina's smooth voice said, full of disdain.

"Nina? What the hell is going on? Is Mac ok?" I asked. Zeb took the phone from me.

"Nina, it's Zeb, I'm here with Cricket. What have you done with Mac?" Oh my God. Nina, an alpha predator who drank blood to survive, had my teenage daughter. What the hell was she going to do with her? I was fighting back tears, listening as Zeb spoke to Nina.

"Oh, she's fine. But after you and Cricket pulled that stunt last night, leaving me alone to fight off those witches, I figured I needed some extra insurance," she said, with a hollow laugh. "Cricket, I need your help. I need this curse lifted, and fast. My time is running out, and when my time is up, so is your daughter's. Are we clear?" Nina's velvety smooth voice was crystal clear over the phone and my heart froze in my chest.

How the hell was I supposed to help her? I knew nothing about curses, much less lifting one. I already showed her all the addresses I had delivered to that day, and she'd already confronted the witches at the address where I'd delivered the mystery package. What more could I possibly do?

I took a deep breath. "I don't know what else I can do to help, Nina. Tell me, what can I do? I swear,

I'll do whatever I can to help you just please, don't hurt my daughter." I suppressed a sob, not wanting to let her hear me cry. And if Mac was listening, I wanted her to know I was staying strong for her.

After a moment of silence, I heard Nina chuckle. I looked at Zeb in confusion. He shrugged and looked away. "You don't know, do you?" she said.

"Know what?" I asked, once again looking to Zeb for help. He didn't meet my eyes. What was she talking about?

"There's no time to go into it now, just know that you can indeed help me, as no one else can. The curse has made me mortal again and I'm already aging. I have little time left. I can't find Aaron, I don't know how he's faring and I'm worried," she said, her voice cracking slightly at that.

"Cricket, you are the only one who can help me and if you want your daughter to survive, I suggest that you agree. *Now*," Nina added in an icy voice.

Without missing a beat, I said, "I'll help you! I'll help you, let me know where and when and what to do. But give me your word you won't hurt her." Zeb put his arms around me at that and I let him, grateful for the support. I sank into him as the gravity of the situation set in.

"I'll text you an address shortly. Don't disappoint me," she said and hung up.

Chapter 18

After receiving the address from Nina via text, we headed towards downtown Nashville. It was the middle of the day and I was curious whether Nina still had an aversion to sunlight now since Edward's death had activated the curse. Zeb was driving my car, and I sat in the passenger seat, lost in thought. We still had some time before we were to meet her. My mind kept returning to Nina's words... *You don't know, do you?*

"Zeb, what did Nina mean when she said, 'you don't know'?" Zeb had his eyes fixed on the road ahead and did not meet my gaze. His knuckles went white as he gripped the steering wheel and he was quiet for a few moments before he answered.

Finally, he sighed and cleared his throat. "About that. It's probably not a good time to chat about it, honestly. But since she brought it up and we're in this bloody situation we're in now, I guess I've got no choice but to tell you." He risked a peek at me, then returned his gaze to the road.

My eyes widened. "You know what she's talking about? You know something about me, both of you do, and no one thought to tell me about it?" I said, my voice growing louder with every word. I stared at him, waiting.

"I would say don't freak out, but it looks like I've left it too late for that," he said.

"TELL ME. I want to know before we get there since she's expecting me to help her somehow," I said, reining it in a bit, hoping to convince him to spit it out.

He sighed again. "You are what we call a Revealer in the supernatural world," he said, pulling the car into an empty parking lot and bringing it to a stop.

I stared blankly at him. "What the hell does that mean?"

"It means that you can sense magic and supernatural powers when you're near them." He ran one hand through his hair and the corners of his mouth turned down in a frown as he continued. "It's how you knew the house on Caldwell was the right one when Nina took you there. It's also why the vampires took an interest in you and wanted you working for them. They knew your ability would come in handy at some point," he said, finally turning to look at me with a pained expression.

"A *Revealer*? Why does that sound like the lamest supernatural power ever? And if it's true, how come I never knew about it?" I asked incredulously, crossing my arms and scowling at him.

My first instinct was to call bullshit and ask him to take me to the police. Frankly, I'd had about enough of all this supernatural crap and I just wanted my old life back. For a moment, I imagined myself bursting into the police station and explaining that a vampire had kidnapped my daughter because she was trying to force me to help her lift the curse on her. They'd likely arrest me, or throw me in a mental hospital. So yeah, that wouldn't work.

I leaned back in the seat and closed my eyes. Just a few short weeks ago, I would've told you that vampires were not real, and the Grim Reaper was a myth too. However, I had since learned they were both very real and they weren't the only supernatural creatures out there, either. If this Revealer stuff was true too, then I needed to understand it; I needed to know what it meant.

Zeb smiled weakly at me. "On the surface, it may seem *lame* as you call it. It's a powerful gift, though, Cricket. Think about all the supernatural beings out there, some you don't even know about yet, that don't want to be found. They want to stay hidden away, kept a secret from humans and other supernaturals who may mean to harm them. A Revealer is their worst nightmare," he said, taking my hand. I looked away but let him continue holding my hand, which he squeezed gently.

"We think it had lain dormant in you until something triggered it recently. It has probably been in your family for generations but never activated. We don't know what the catalyst was yet, but there are some theories which we don't have time to get into now. What we know is that Revealers are rare and powerful; and that puts them in significant danger," he stated, rubbing the back of my hand with his thumb as he spoke.

I pulled my hand from his. "What do you mean, *we*?"

He pursed his lips and ran a hand through his blond hair. "The reason my employers sent me here was to protect you and keep you alive. You're a Revealer which is a very rare and important gift and once word spreads in the supernatural community about you…" he trailed off and a shiver ran down my spine.

"I'm not sure exactly how the vampires found out about you, but once they did, they wasted no time in putting you on the payroll." He stared off into the distance for a moment before turning to pin me with his sparkling blue eyes.

"Cricket, that may be why they sent me here in the beginning but it's not why I'm here now. I need you to know that. There's something about you…" He tilted his head as he spoke and his expression softened.

"I care about you. You, not your gift, just you," he said, brushing an errant hair away from my face, tucking it behind my ear. He cupped my jaw and traced my lower lip with his thumb.

I could get lost in those ice-blue eyes, that gentle touch. I leaned into him. There was something about him too. Was it only these mysterious Revealer abilities that drew me to him?

His hand slid to my neck, pulling me to him and closing the space between us. His lips found mine, and I met his kiss with one of my own. Zeb sighed my name and held my face as the kiss deepened. I felt a kaleidoscope of butterflies fluttering in my stomach, all because of this man.

Can I trust him? I wondered. I closed my eyes and sighed, leaning forward and letting my forehead rest against his. I wanted to believe I could trust him, with my heart and with getting Mac back safely, too.

I saw the way he was gazing at me. This hardened biker—who also was a Grim Reaper—leather clad, with tattoos, spiky blond hair, silver rings on every finger, and a resting bitch face that could send Satan himself running. This guy was staring at me right now with an expression so soft, it was the polar opposite of what his exterior said about him. And I did that to him. Me.

Yes, I could trust him.

We found Nina waiting for us at an abandoned warehouse in Bordeaux, a seedy part of Nashville. The parking lot was empty, except for the white utility van Nina stood next to, with an annoyed expression on her face. She checked her watch and scowled at me as we pulled in next to the van.

I practically jumped out of the car before Zeb even put it in park. "Where is she?" I demanded, slamming the door behind me and rushing to the van.

Nina smirked, her hateful red lips curling into a grin. "She's fine. And she'll stay that way if you cooperate," she said, arms crossed in front of her.

I stopped to look at her—really look at her. Her formerly jet-black hair was shot with gray now. Her skin didn't look as bright and smooth, in fact it hung from her frame. The most notable difference, though, were her eyes. No longer the rich whiskey color of vampires, they were now a dull brown. The curse was real; Nina was a mere mortal again. And I knew it was killing her in more ways than one.

"I want to see her before I do anything," I stated, hands on hips with Zeb towering next to me.

Nina narrowed her eyes. "I just told you, she's fine. We don't have time for this," she said.

I smirked. "Correction. *You* don't have time for this, do you? We have plenty of time. Let me see her. NOW."

Zeb stepped forward. "Nina, if you want Cricket's help, we need to know that she's not being harmed. We'll wait while you decide," he said while cracking his knuckles.

157

She winced and pulled her long black coat a little tighter. "Harmed? I would never harm her, I'm appalled that you would think that," she sputtered.

Zeb and I stood in place, and I crossed my arms while glaring at her.

She sighed. "Fine. Chad, open the door," she called out and obediently, Chad hopped out and opened the large side door of the van.

And there she was, my baby girl, sitting inside the van on the floor. Hands tied behind her back, her eyes blindfolded. She was wearing black jeans and a black t-shirt, her usual attire. I could see tear streaks on her dirty face, and I felt a fury rise within me I had never known before in my life. I instinctively made for the van with a sob when Chad appeared in front of me, pointing a gun in Mac's direction. I immediately stopped in my tracks.

"Mac, baby, I'm here!" I called, my voice strangled with unshed tears and rage. I felt Zeb's arms wrap around me as we both watched Chad twirling the gun in his hands with a sneer on his face.

"Mom!" I heard her call out, trying to rise from her seated position. With one last taunting grin, Chad slammed the side door of the van shut. Then he turned his pistol on me.

I could still hear her crying and screaming while Zeb held me back from running to the van. I wanted to rip the door off, and I thought I could do it. My entire body felt like it was on fire, burning with anger and fury. I didn't care that Chad was pointing the pistol directly at me now, but Zeb did. He kept a hold on me until I gained enough control to speak to Nina.

Finally, I turned to her. She was leaning against the building, studying her nails. "Satisfied? Can we get back to business now?" she asked, looking up at me with a smirk.

I grabbed Zeb's hand and squeezed it tightly. He squeezed back, just as tightly. "I will help you and you will return her to me safely," I said in a frosty voice as I glowered at Nina. "I swear if you touch one hair on her head—"

"I promise, Cricket. I will not harm her. As long as you hold up your end of the bargain," Nina said, narrowing her eyes at me.

"Let's get this over with then."

Chapter 19

About forty-five minutes later, we found ourselves back in front of the house on Caldwell, where the witches lived. Since Nina had already made their acquaintance and would likely not be welcomed back, she stayed in the car while Zeb and I approached the porch. I rang the doorbell and waited. Again, I felt the strange sensations I felt before, a general sense of uneasiness and foreboding. I guessed that was my newfound spidey senses kicking in.

After a few moments, the girl, who I'd previously dubbed Bellatrix, opened the door. Surprised at first, her mouth quickly twisted into a haughty grin. "Back for more? Where's your friend?" she asked in that Jersey accent, craning her neck to peer around us.

"First of all, she's not my friend. And yes, we're back because we need information. I'm Cricket, by the way, and this is Zeb," I said, gesturing to towards him.

"Don't care." Her glossy, black lips formed into a sneer as she tried to shut the door in our faces. God, she reminded me of Mac. I quickly reached out to grab the door just before it closed.

"Please. My teenage daughter's life is at stake here. Nina—the woman I was with before—she has my daughter and she will kill her unless I help her get the answers she needs. Please, would you answer a few questions?" I pleaded. Her face seemed to soften a bit after hearing me out. "What's your name?" I ventured.

She couldn't have been over sixteen or seventeen herself. Maybe I had gotten through to her? I could feel the energy around us changing, the uneasiness was lifting. There was still an electricity in the air that I could feel, but it wasn't giving off the same bad vibes as before. Was it the girl's energy I was picking up on all along?

Her grip on the door relaxed. "I'm Regina," she said, eying me and then Zeb. "I guess I could answer a few questions. No promises though," she said, opening the door wide enough to allow us inside.

"Thank you, Regina," I said, giving her a grateful smile as she let us in. I looked around the spacious living room she led us into. I saw the candles I had spotted before. The room was bleak, decorated in blacks, grays, and ominous reds. Who was this girl's mother, Morticia Addams? Mac would love it, I thought. Oh, Mac.

She indicated we should sit down on a black tufted loveseat while she sat in a gray Victorian parlor chair across from us, with a glass coffee table in between. Zeb arranged his tall, muscular form carefully on the tiny loveseat, which I found amusing despite everything. I sat in the small space left beside him.

"Like, what do you want to know?" Regina said, skipping the small talk. She glanced around, probably looking to see if Robbie was anywhere within earshot. I wondered who he was to her and how he would feel about this. Best to get down to it and get out of here as quickly as possible, I thought.

"I unwittingly delivered a package here a few days ago. I don't remember if you took the delivery or if someone else did. Do you remember anything about it? Who did the package ultimately end up with? Do you know what was in it?" I fired questions at her, and Zeb placed a hand on my knee and squeezed softly, as if to say, "Easy, Tiger". He was right, I didn't want her to kick us out because I was being too aggressive, so I stopped myself from asking anything else for now.

Again, she checked behind her and then looked back at us warily. "My brother, Robbie, took the package. He didn't open it in front of me, so I don't know what was in it." She followed up in a softer voice and said, "Another vampire was here too. I think he has something to do with all of this, but I'm not sure how."

Holy smokes, now we're getting somewhere.

"Another vampire? Male or female? Did you get their name?" Zeb asked Regina before I could. I leaned forward in my seat. I could tell he was as excited as I was that we were finally getting some useful information to help free my daughter.

"It was a man. I think I heard Robbie call him Ron, or something like that. I didn't get a good look at him. He wasn't here long. Then they left together and took the package with them," Regina shrugged, continuing in hushed tones. "Look, that's all I should say. I don't want to get myself in trouble. But I hope you get your daughter back, Cricket." She offered a sympathetic smile.

That's all we're getting out of her, I realized with some disappointment. I stood, Zeb followed suit, and I reached out my hand to Regina.

"You've been an enormous help, Regina, we appreciate it," Zeb said.

"I'm sorry for all the trouble the other night; Nina isn't really a people person," I added.

Regina's mouth quirked up into a wry smile as she took my hand. As she did, I felt the flow of her energy run through me. No longer dark and foreboding, I still felt a twinge of anxiety from her. She's probably

163

worried about Robbie finding out she talked to us. This supernatural radar detector stuff would take some getting used to.

Regina shut the door behind us, and we made our way down the stairs slowly. I was hoping for a few moments alone with Zeb to discuss what we'd learned and to get his thoughts on who Ron could be, but Nina jumped out of the car almost immediately upon seeing us emerge from the house.

"Well, what did she say?" Nina demanded.

"She said you're a—" I started, but Zeb interrupted me. Probably a good thing.

"She gave us some useful information, Nina. Do you know anyone named Ron?" Zeb said, standing by the car with hands on hips.

Nina scowled. "No, I don't know anyone named Ron. Don't tell me that's all you got out of her?"

"Regina, that's the witch you *met* last time we were here," I said, as Nina rolled her eyes. "She said that her brother, Robbie, took delivery of the package. She also said that another vampire, she thought his name was Ron, came by and Robbie and he left together. They took the package with them and she didn't know what was inside," I said, summarizing the conversation before Nina could go ballistic on us.

Nina sighed with exasperation, throwing her hands up in the air. "Well, what now?"

I sighed and looked at the ground. I really didn't know what to do next if Nina didn't know who the hell Ron was. I looked at Zeb for guidance.

Thankfully, he spoke up. "We're going to find bloody Robbie and follow him. See if he goes to meet this Ron bloke again."

More surveillance. More amateur detective work. I just wanted to take Mac home. Hell, I'd even go back to Abernathy, Smith, and Sanchez and beg for my job back if it meant I could wash my hands of these supernatural freaks and their drama forever. But that ship had sailed, seeing as I was now one of those supernatural freaks myself, it seemed.

No one objected, so Zeb continued. "Alright, then. We get in the car and drive away in case Regina is watching. We'll park a couple streets over and I'll come back on foot to watch for Robbie," Zeb said. He took my hand and squeezed it, a gesture that did not go unnoticed by Nina. She raised her eyebrows at us.

"I want to come back with you to watch for Robbie," I said, to which Nina began shaking her head.

She coughed a little, and I noticed some blood at the corners of her mouth. "No. Cricket stays with me. I won't have you two running off and leaving me," she said.

Zeb argued, but I placed a hand on his arm to stop him. "It's fine, I'll stay. She's mortal now," I said, and she glared at me. "It's not like she can drain my blood or anything," I continued, twisting the knife a little deeper. I hated to admit it, but I was enjoying her discomfort at being human again.

We all got back into the car and Zeb drove us a few streets away, parked inconspicuously, and headed back to Regina's house on foot. The plan was he would text me when he saw Robbie so I could drive back over to pick him up, then we would tail Robbie.

I was sad to see him go, but I definitely enjoyed the view as he walked away, wearing those tight-fitting black jeans. I bit my lip as he jogged down the street. Then Nina's irritating voice snapped me out of it.

"So, you and the Reaper? How romantic," she said, her voice dripping with derision. She began coughing again and dug in her purse for a silk handkerchief which she used to dab at her mouth. I watched in silence. There was a time I might have felt sympathy for her, as she had been a decent employer. Or had seemed to be at the time, anyway. Not now. This bitch was holding my daughter hostage. As far as I was concerned now, she could rot in hell.

"Yeah, not nearly as romantic as having an affair with your husband's son, though," I said, crossing my arms and looking out the window.

Nina barked out a laugh. "You have no idea what it was like being married to Edward," she said. She was quiet for a few moments, as if she were reminiscing, then she began again.

"In the beginning it was amazing. He was younger. We had fun together. Every night was a different party; we defined the social scene in Nashville in those days," she said, wistfully. "As time went on, his business became more successful and he made more money. Lots of money. So much money that it changed him. He became paranoid that I only wanted him for his fortune, which wasn't true. At least it wasn't true back then." She stared out the window as if she had forgotten I was even in the car with her. I couldn't help myself, I continued to listen in case she dropped any valuable information.

"He grew cold and distant; he didn't trust me. I was lonely. He refused to allow me to turn him, and he continued to age, as humans do. The years passed by

166

and we grew further apart. Then Aaron moved back to Nashville, and he was like his father used to be, back in the old days. He was young, full of energy, full of passion. It happened. I blame Edward for letting it happen." She coughed again and dabbed her mouth with her handkerchief before continuing.

"He saw that Aaron and I were becoming closer and he did nothing. He forbade me to turn his son, never mind the fact that Aaron wanted to be turned. With Edward, his wants and needs were the only thing that mattered. He didn't care what anyone else wanted," she said, ending with another coughing fit that lasted a few minutes this time.

I sighed and remained silent. What did she want me to say? I had no sympathy for her; she'd made her own bed. After she finished, she wiped the blood and spittle from her mouth.

"So where is Aaron now? Why isn't he helping you?"

She glared at me and didn't answer. Interesting. Her precious Aaron was MIA, apparently.

"Isn't he cursed with mortality now too? Why wouldn't he want to work with you to lift the curse, to return you both to immortality? For that matter, why can't you just find another vampire to turn you again?" I snapped at her, tired of her playing the victim.

"It doesn't work that way, Cricket," she spat. "Don't you think I would've done that already? I can't be turned again. Technically, I'm still a vampire, without the immortality. And Aaron, he's—" the sound of my phone cut her off, the long-awaited text from Zeb.

"He spotted Robbie, we need to go," I said, relieved I didn't have to listen to any more of her ramblings. I started the car and headed back to Regina's house.

Chapter 20

I slowed down to let Zeb jump into the passenger seat. "Take a right, we should be able to catch him," he said. I had a scowl on my face, as a result of being alone with Nina while we waited. He glanced at me with a raised eyebrow, and then at Nina in the backseat. I gave him a quick shrug and turned my attention to the road.

I drove at a fast pace until I saw a black sedan up ahead and Zeb shouted, "That's him!" I slowed and allowed another car to get between us while keeping an eye on the sedan and where it was going.

We followed for several miles and many turns until finally we pulled into a posh gated neighborhood. Nina, who had been sulking quietly, sat straight up in the backseat and looked out the window. "Why are we here?" she asked.

Zeb and I looked at each other. She should know very well what we're doing here. Was her memory going now that she was mortal again and aging rapidly?

"Why is he taking us to Aaron's house?" Nina said. Oh. Well, that was an interesting development.

Then it hit me. "Ron" must be Aaron. I almost laughed out loud. Could Aaron have turned on Nina? Is he out to lift the curse, but only for himself? Wouldn't that be something, I thought.

I couldn't resist. I twisted in the seat so I could turn to look at Nina in the back. "Looks like Aaron is finding his own solution—without you," I said and turned back to the road. I noticed Zeb's disapproving look in my peripheral vision, which I interpreted as "Shut up, Cricket". He was right. It didn't matter though, because she didn't seem to have heard me. In the rearview mirror, I watched her take phone out of her bag and dial.

Zeb indicated where I should park, down the street from where Robbie's sedan pulled into the driveway of a huge two-story house. He risked a glance at Nina, saw her on her phone, and said, "What the bloody hell are you doing? Are you daft, woman? We're trying to be discreet here."

She punched the end button and tossed the phone back into her purse. "He's not answering anyway," she said in a huff.

"Alright, I'm going to spy on them and see what I can find out," I said. I took my cross-body bag off and sat it on the floorboard.

"Cricket—" Zeb began shaking his head, but I cut him off.

"I want to bring Mac home. Today. If that means taking some risks, that's what I'll do. I can't expect you to take all the risks for me," I said, opening the car door and jumping out before Zeb could say anything further on the subject.

He was faster than I gave him credit for. He was out of the car and had me by the elbow before I knew it, turning me to face him. "I'll gladly take all the risks for you, and for Mac," he said, cupping my face.

I shook my head. "I appreciate that, Zeb, I do, but I can't let you. Besides, I've already babysat *her* once, it's your turn," I said, jerking my head in Nina's direction. "I'm sick of her. I'm sick of vampires and witches and—" I stopped and looked at Zeb, who was staring at me with amusement.

"Grim Reapers?" he asked, the corner of his mouth twitching.

I rolled my eyes. "The Grim Reaper I know has actually managed not to be a pain in the ass today. But he's walking on thin ice," I said with a smirk.

He took my hand and looked at me earnestly. "Be careful, Princess. Don't linger and hurry back." I nodded, and Zeb released me.

I walked up the drive of the neighboring house, glancing around to make sure no one was watching me. I walked between the houses and into Aaron's back yard. I peeked into a couple of windows, but I couldn't see anything. I kept going, creeping from one window to the next, until I reached what appeared to be the living room. I could barely make out two forms inside, but I could hear their muffled voices.

"You know who I'm talking about, Aaron. That bitch was at our house. I'm tired of this, I want my share of the money, now," came the voice of Robbie, I was guessing, the Jersey accent just as thick as his sister's.

I moved so I remained hidden but had a little better view inside the house. Aaron was standing while Robbie sat on the couch. Aaron had a drink in his hand, which he threw back before he faced Robbie.

"You'll get your money when I get this curse lifted. That was the deal. There's not a lot of time left, how's the old man coming with it?" Aaron asked, running his hands through his hair.

Robbie sighed. "He's almost got it. Shouldn't be long now," he said. "In the meantime, keep your girlfriend away from us. I don't want her near Regina again," he warned.

Aaron waved a hand dismissively. "She won't be an issue for much longer," he said, pouring himself another drink, and adding, "She's not my girlfriend, either."

Robbie closed the distance between himself and Aaron until their noses were nearly touching. For a moment they stood like that, as if they were having a silent staring contest. Robbie was tall and fit, with light brown skin, short black hair, and blue eyes. A perfect contrast to Aaron's lanky, pale form with whiskey-colored eyes and light brown hair. Robbie was hot, I had to admit. As I was about to give up and head back to the car, I saw Aaron grab Robbie's neck to pull him closer as he planted his lips firmly on Robbie's.

I couldn't wait to tell Nina about this, I thought with glee. The kiss deepened as Aaron's hands went around Robbie's waist, pulling Robbie roughly to him. Robbie's hands wandered over Aaron's back and hips as their kisses became more passionate and they collapsed onto the sofa.

I thought it was time for me to return to the car. I crept away from the house and back down the driveway of the neighboring home, retracing my steps back to the car down the street.

Zeb was leaning on the car when I approached. Apparently, he'd had enough of Nina too. She'd probably said something that made him choose between standing outside the car or killing her, and luckily for her, he chose the former.

"Alright?" he asked, and I nodded.

We got back into the car at about the same time. Zeb started the engine, and we were off with Nina leaning forward to ask, "What happened?" She burst into a coughing fit just then, which gave me time to think about what I wanted to reveal right now. Would it be in mine and Mac's interest to tell her what I witnessed? Could I stop myself from telling her if I tried though?

Zeb gave me a questioning look. If only my superpower was telepathy, I thought. But no, the universe had made me the equivalent of a supernatural metal detector. I can't catch a break.

As she finished her coughing spell, I began. "So. I heard Robbie and Aaron talking and it seems like they have someone working on a spell to lift the curse..." I trailed off. Nina looked at me expectantly. Was I a terrible person because I was looking forward to the next part? I'd contemplate that later. I continued, "And it would appear that Robbie and Aaron are—" I paused for dramatic effect. "—involved." I looked at Zeb, whose eyes nearly bulged out of his head at that.

The news went over Nina's head, though. She looked from me to Zeb, then back at me. "Go on, involved in what?" she asked. I suppressed a giggle.

I cleared my throat and bit my lip to keep from smiling. "Involved with each other. Involved in sticking their tongues down each other's throats when I left them, to be specific," I said, barely keeping the laughter out of my voice.

"Well, that's an interesting development," Zeb said, not bothering to hide the amusement in his voice.

Nina's jaw dropped open. She closed it after a few moments and looked around the backseat of the car, as if she would find some explanation back there. "That's impossible."

"It's entirely possible. Saw it happen with my own eyes. It was hot, too," I added. That brought a look of disapproval from Zeb as he scowled at me, his brows drawn. Too much, Cricket, I told myself. She still has Mac within her grasp, I can't risk pissing her off too much.

After a few silent moments, I heard Nina sniffle. Oh no, I would not feel sorry for her. Hell no. But before I could say anything else, she spat, "Back to the warehouse. I need to think."

I looked at Zeb, who shrugged and began driving. God, please let Mac be ok, I prayed.

Back at the warehouse, Nina vaulted out of the car almost before it came to a complete stop. I followed as fast as I could, grabbing her by the arm when I reached her. "Hey, I helped you, you know more now than you did. I'm taking Mac home with me, now."

Nina whirled around to face me, an ugly snarl on her face. She looked even older than she had a few hours ago, if that was possible. She barked out a laugh. "Oh Cricket, you're so naïve. You're not done helping me and until the curse has been lifted, she stays with me. I don't care what you must do or who you must go through. Aaron will not save himself and leave me to die!" she screamed that last part, bringing on a coughing fit.

As she coughed and convulsed, I ran for the van and pulled on the door. Locked. I beat on the side of the van. "Chad, open the door! Open it now, you son of a bitch!" I yelled, kicking and screaming. Zeb tried to open the door too, to no avail. I could see Chad smirking at us from the driver's seat, then the van began moving.

"Mom!" I heard a muffled cry from inside. I ran after the van as it drifted away from us and nearer to Nina. I reached the back and pulled on the doors, also locked.

"Damn it!" I cried, punching the back door of the van as hard as I could.

Nina had recovered herself by then. Chad had maneuvered the van until it was right next to Nina. He swung the passenger side door open and slowed down long enough for her to hoist herself up into the seat, slamming the door behind her.

The window rolled down, and she called, "You know how to reach me when you have what I need. Do it. Or else," she said, glaring at me, and I could see tears rolling down her cheeks. "And don't follow us. If you want to keep your daughter alive, that is."

The van took off, leaving us in the dust in the deserted parking lot. I turned to Zeb, sobbing. He wrapped his muscular arms around me, one hand stroking my hair, while he whispered to me.

"We will get her back, Cricket, we will. And Nina will pay, I'll make certain of it," he said as I cried into his shoulder, clutching his shirt in my fists. We stood there in the parking lot like that for a while, with me crying and him stroking my back, my hair, and reassuring me that my daughter was not gone for good.

Finally, my tears subsided enough to speak. "Take me home," I groaned. I walked back to the car, dejected and full of regret and shame. Would Mac ever forgive me for letting this happen to her? If I ever got her back, that is.

We were silent all the way home. Zeb pulled the car into our shared drive, got out, and ran around to the passenger side to open the door for me and help me out. I moved as if I was in a fog. I didn't know what to do now. It all seemed hopeless and despair was setting in.

He walked with me up the stairs and took my keys from me to open the door. The first thing I saw when I walked in was one of Mac's black hoodies slung over the back of the couch and the tears started anew. I sat down on the couch, put my head in my hands, and let the tears come. My heart ached. It felt like she was gone forever. What if I couldn't find what Nina wanted to save herself? What would she do to Mac? The possibilities were more than I could bear to think about.

Zeb sat down beside me and took my hands in his, making me look up at him. "What's this now? We'll get her back, Cricket. Don't doubt it. Whatever I have to do, I will do it. We start again as soon as we can find Robbie tomorrow, we'll follow him everywhere he goes until he leads us to this warlock. We won't fail, alright?" he said, cupping my face with one hand and wiping the tears from my cheek with his thumb.

In that moment, I just needed to believe him. I needed him to tell me it was all going to be okay, that Mac would be okay and I would get her back safely. He was the only thing that made sense right now.

I looked into his eyes, so earnest and full of emotion. For me, and for my daughter, who he barely knew. I could feel waves of comfort and peace coming from him now that I was letting myself feel something more than my own despair. He really cared for me, I realized.

I leaned in and kissed him, slow and soft at first with our lips pressing together tentatively, almost shyly. He kissed me back and after a few moments, there was an urgency in our kisses. No longer gentle, I let my hands wander into his hair, down his back, pulling him closer.

His hands roamed over my arms, shoulders, my back, my hips, then back again as we continued to kiss. I wanted to lose myself in this moment here with him, safe with him. His hand crept up inside the front of my shirt and stroked my breast, eliciting a moan from me. I felt him smile against my mouth for a moment. He kissed me deeply once more and pulled back to look at me.

I caught my breath and raised an eyebrow. "What?" I asked.

He drew me close again and pressed his forehead against mine. "I want you. I want you so badly, Cricket. But not like this, not when you're overcome with grief and pain and you're looking for a way to dull it for a while. I want you so much that I'm willing to wait until every emotion you're feeling is because of me, because of us," he breathed, pushing a stray hair out of my face and behind my ear.

"Oh." I said, not sure how I felt about that. I wanted him right now. How could he refuse me? But he had a point about how I was feeling.

I sighed and sagged into his embrace. "You're right... damn it, you're right."

He chuckled, cupping my face once again and kissed me lightly. "Let's put you to bed, you need some rest. We have work to do tomorrow," he said, pulling me to my feet. We climbed the stairs to my bedroom, where I was so tired that I simply took off my shoes and crawled into bed as I was. Zeb leaned down to kiss me and turned to go.

"Hey," I called as he reached the bedroom door, his hand on the light switch. "Will you stay with me? Just until I fall asleep," I asked in a small voice, afraid he would refuse.

He didn't answer, instead I felt the bed creak a few moments later with the weight of him. He slid under the covers behind me, wrapping me in his embrace.

"Goodnight, Cricket," he said, planting a kiss on my neck.

"Goodnight, Zeb," I said and closed my eyes.

Chapter 21

I woke alone the next morning, and I had several voice mails waiting on my phone. First was Grandma, wanting to know why I hadn't been by Forever Young and how Mac and I were doing. Big sigh. The next one was from Doreen, excitedly chatting away about our new jobs, telling me she wanted to have lunch before Monday to discuss. Even bigger sigh. Lastly, Joey had left a message. It was vague; he said he needed to see me soon. That one piqued my interest.

Could he possibly have some information that would help? I decided there was no time like the present to find out. By now, it was late morning, as I had slept a long time after the exhausting events of the previous day. I showered and dressed quickly while my coffee was brewing and decided I would visit Joey in person at The Rusty Nail for a late lunch.

As I headed out, I noticed Zeb's bike was gone. Weird. I wondered where he was, then remembered his job. Maybe he was on another "house call"? I decided I'd just text him and let him know I was meeting Joey at the Nail because of his voice message and that I was hoping maybe he could help us.

By the time I got there, the place was empty as most of the lunch crowd headed out and back to work, or whatever it was they did during the day. A few stragglers were still dining, and the jukebox was playing "Livin' On A Prayer" by Bon Jovi. I spotted Joey at the bar, and he smiled when he saw me. He was in bartender attire, which entailed a white t-shirt, an apron, and jeans. Somehow, he still looked sexy, I thought.

179

As I walked closer to him, I sensed something, like static electricity in the air. What the hell was that? Was my supernatural sonar on the fritz? Clearly, I needed to find someone who could tell me more about this so-called gift and how it worked, and soon.

"Cricket, I'm glad you stopped by. Give me a minute and I'll join you at a booth so we can talk," Joey said while mixing drinks for two guys at the bar. Day drinkers, I salute you, I thought, taking a seat at a nearby booth. I ordered an appetizer when the waitress came by and checked my phone. Nothing from Zeb or anyone else. I wondered if he was already tracking Robbie.

After a few moments, Joey joined me. He sat down in the seat opposite me at the booth and asked, "What's been going on?"

I sighed. Where to start? "Oh, let's see. I got promoted." I paused, not sure what to say next.

"That's great!" he said, reaching across the table to squeeze my hand. "So, things are going well at Sunshine, then?" he asked.

The waitress brought my loaded fries, and I didn't hesitate to dig in after offering some to Joey, which he declined.

While we made small talk, and I ate, the static electricity I had felt upon entering the bar had grown stronger and steadier. After he had taken my hand, it felt like a current of electricity was flowing all around my body. Not necessarily unpleasant, but different. Something was up.

I finished my food and looked around to see if anyone was paying attention to us. There was only one couple left at a table across the room, polishing off their plates of chicken wings. And the guys at the bar, watching a game on television. I looked at Joey carefully and as I did, his face grew serious.

"Real talk, Joey?"

"Sure? What's up?" he said, looking worried. He also looked around the bar, then back at me.

"This will sound weird, but—what the hell are you?" I blurted.

He sputtered, avoiding my gaze. "What do you mean, 'what am I'?" he asked. The electricity surged around me. I was onto something.

I sighed. "Joey, I recently found out I have a gift. Somehow, I can detect supernatural beings and activity. And I'm detecting some crazy shit around you. Spill it."

He laughed nervously, looking around. "I don't know what you're talking about. You can detect what now?"

I gave him a "cut the bullshit" look, and he finally leveled his gaze at me. He looked at the floor and rubbed the back of his neck before finally meeting my eyes again.

"Alright. Look, only a couple people around here know about me. Most of my family live in Kentucky and Ohio and to my knowledge, I'm the only one in Nashville," he whispered.

"The only one what?" I said, holding my breath. Oh my God, I had been right! This little gift might not be all bad, I thought.

"Werewolf," he whispered.

My eyes widened, and I gasped. A werewolf? Joey? No way.

"What? Really?"

He leaned back in his chair. "You wanted to know, now you know. I'm assuming you know about the vampires at Sunshine Cleaners, then? That's why I wasn't crazy about you working for them. I had no idea you were a Revealer," he said, eying me warily.

"*I* had no idea I was a Revealer until recently," I said. I fiddled with the hem of the tablecloth. "Look, I've got a problem, and I was hoping maybe you could help somehow. Thank you for telling me the truth, by the way," I added. He smiled that cute little crooked grin of his and cocked his head to the side.

"What kind of problem?" he asked. So, I told him everything; about work at Sunshine, Carl's job offer, Nina's confession about Edward and the curse, and Mac. Everything.

His face hardened as I finished. "Where is Nina?"

"Settle down," I said, holding one hand up as he clenched his jaw. I could see subtle changes in the irises of his eyes, which both intrigued and terrified me now that I knew what he was. "Zeb and I are working on getting Nina what she wants. We've got it handled, I just wanted to know if you had any useful information," I added.

He didn't look convinced as he rubbed his chin stubble, with a contemplative look on his face. "Zeb, huh? You sure you can trust him?"

Before I could answer, the door to The Nail swung open and there was Zeb with an agitated look on his face. That look only increased in intensity when he spotted Joey and I sitting in a booth together. I put on a smile and waved him over, which seemed to smooth things over a bit as he walked towards us.

Joey made a huffing sound when he saw Zeb and said, "Doesn't he let you go anywhere without him?"

"Be nice," I whispered seconds before Zeb slid into the seat, slipping an arm around me. He planted a kiss on my cheek, which raised Joey's eyebrow. *Someone wants to establish dominance,* I thought, with an internal chuckle.

"Mate," Zeb said, nodding at Joey.

"Hey man," Joey said back. *This is not awkward at all.*

"Find out anything?" I asked, turning to Zeb. He gave me a questioning look, then shot a glance at Joey. "I filled him in already. Turns out he had a secret of his own that I figured out. He's a—" but Joey cut me off.

"Zeb already knows, and I know about him too," Joey said with a shrug.

I narrowed my eyes at them both. "Fine. Did you find Robbie?" I asked, turning my attention back to Zeb.

He nodded. "I did. I attached a tracking device to his car. I've been watching it and the bloke's not done anything except go to Starbucks and the gas station so far."

I turned back to Joey. "Okay, you've had time to think. Do you know anything at all that might help us?"

"I know Robbie and Aaron have been seeing each other for quite a while. They've been in the bar together before. That's about it," he said. I must have had a disappointed look on my face because he added, "Werewolves without a pack tend to keep to themselves," and shrugged.

I sighed. So much for that. "Alright, so we keep watching the tracker and the minute it looks like Robbie is going somewhere interesting, we follow him," I said to Zeb.

His phone made a chirping noise, and he took it out and checked the screen. "Speak of the devil, Princess," he said. "Right, looks like we need to go."

Joey looked at me in horror and mouthed "Princess?" I suppressed a laugh.

"We'll talk soon, Joe. Call me if you think of anything that might help," I said, rising to follow Zeb, who had already made it to the door.

Joey grabbed my elbow as I turned to go. "So, you and the Reaper, huh? Be careful with him, Cricket. I've heard things, okay? And I'm not just saying that because I'm jealous, which I am." He smiled that adorable crooked grin of his again. "Promise me?"

"I'll be careful, I promise," I said, squeezing his hand and turning to follow Zeb.

In the car on the way to catch up to Robbie, Zeb finally said, "I'm not sure telling him everything was a good shout."

I looked at Zeb, confused. "Who, Joey? Why not?"

"I don't trust werewolves. Especially lone wolves," he said, as if that explained everything.

I sighed. "I've known Joey for years. He's fine."

"Werewolves are meant to be in packs, that he's alone here tells me there's something wrong." He glanced at me before continuing. "Just be careful around him, Princess," Zeb said, steering the car into a turn.

I laughed. "Funny, he said the same thing about you," I said. He scowled.

I caught sight of the black sedan up ahead of us, there were a few cars in between. Zeb kept us at a distance, but still within view of him. We followed for about thirty minutes before I realized that the scenery was looking familiar. Was he taking us to—no, he couldn't be taking us there? What business would Robbie have there? I thought to myself.

"Zeb, Forever Young is just a few blocks away. That's the senior center where Grandma and Gus live. You don't think he's going there, do you?" I asked.

Before Zeb could answer, Robbie answered the question for us by pulling into the parking lot at Forever Young. We kept driving, not wanting to be conspicuous.

"Bloody hell, now what do we do? We can't just follow the bloke inside," Zeb said, running one hand through his blond hair as we sped by.

"I have an idea," I said, pulling my phone out of my bag and pulling up my contacts. After a few moments, she answered. "Grandma, it's Cricket. I need your help."

Zeb grimaced, and I bit my lip to keep from laughing while I put her on speakerphone. "Listen, don't ask questions now, I'll fill you in later. For now, I need you to go to the front desk. There's a guy who should be walking in any minute now and I need to know who he's there to visit." I looked at Zeb, who was shaking his head.

"He's a tall black man, maybe in his mid to late twenties, has black hair and blue eyes. He's probably wearing jeans and a t-shirt," I said.

"He sounds handsome. What should I say to him when I see him?" Grandma asked, sounding excited to be involved in a secret mission.

"Don't talk to him, Grandma! Just try to find out who he's there to see and call me back when you can. Don't let him know that you're watching him. Okay?" I waited for her to agree.

"Alright, dear, I can do that. Wait, hold on a minute," she said, and I heard muffled sounds on the other end of the line, like maybe she had stuck the phone into her pocket or something. Zeb glanced at me, puzzled, and I shrugged.

A few moments later, she was back on the line and whispering, "I'm not sure who this fella is, but a young man just knocked on our door who looks an awful lot like what you described. He's here to see Gus."

Chapter 22

"Now what?" I asked Zeb. I wondered if we should confront Robbie and Gus. What the hell did Gus have to do with this, anyway? Could this be some random coincidence?

Zeb was silent for a few moments while he rubbed the beard stubble on his chin and cheeks. "I think we have to go over there and find out what he's on about," he finally said.

So, we drove back to Forever Young, parked around back, and made our way into the building to Grandma and Gus's room, according to the directions she gave over the phone. Nothing seemed to be out of the ordinary, so I knocked, and Grandma answered the door so quickly I wondered if she had been standing there waiting for us.

She threw the door open and announced, "He just left! I tried to call you back, but maybe I didn't do it right," she said, staring warily at the smart phone in her hand.

I sighed. "Where's Gus? Do you know what Robbie wanted with him?" We entered the living quarters and Grandma showed us to the couch.

"I don't know, but he left with a manila envelope," she said. "Gus hasn't been out of his office since, so I haven't had a chance to ask him."

"Do you think we could speak with him now?" Zeb asked.

Grandma made a face and said, "Oh, I don't know. He doesn't like it when I disturb him while he works."

I drew a deep breath and said, "I don't want to alarm you, but Mac is sort of in some—" I paused before continuing, "—trouble. We've been tracking Robbie, the guy who was here, and if he visited with Gus, there's a good chance that he has some information that could help us."

Grandma's eyes went wide, and she clutched the strand of pearls around her neck. Only Grandma would wear pearls with a purple velour tracksuit that read "juicy" across the ass.

"Trouble? Why didn't you tell me sooner! What kind of trouble? Did that boy, Luther, knock her up?" Grandma scowled at me, already blaming me for this imaginary teenage pregnancy scenario.

"What? No! There's not enough time to explain right now. Look, I'm just going to go knock on his office door," I said, barging past Grandma as she objected.

"Cricket come back here! I swear, that girl has no manners. God knows, I tried." I heard her muttering as Zeb and I swept past her and through the kitchenette, until we reached a closed bedroom door.

I felt a strange sensation while standing in front of it. There was a powerful aura of energy emanating from inside the room, nearly overpowering me. I stumbled back into Zeb and tried to regain my balance. This could only mean one thing.

"Zeb, my spidey senses are tingling. Do you know anything about Gus you should tell me? NOW?" I whispered, narrowing my gaze at him.

"I promise, I don't know anything more than you do, Princess," he said, easing me behind him as he knocked on the door.

Grandma came up behind us just as Gus flung the door open. "I told you, Betty, never disturb me while I'm at work!" he bellowed in a gruff voice, scowling. When he saw us, his expression turned into one of surprise, then panic.

He tried to shut the door, but Zeb caught it before he could. I could see various books and what appeared to be chemistry paraphernalia littering the desk inside.

"Gus? We need a word," I said. Grandma threw her hands up in the air.

We convinced Gus to come out of his office and join us at the little table in the kitchenette. Rather, Zeb threatened him, so Gus decided it was in his best interest to come out. Grandma had set a kettle of water to boil for tea and Zeb and I sat opposite Gus at the table.

He wore the same fedora hat and sunglasses that he had worn the first time I had met him. He crossed his arms, and he looked away from us in a huff. I felt the energy rolling off him, so I knew this man was something more than human. But what? And did Grandma know?

"Look Gus, I'm just gonna get to the point. My daughter is in danger and I think you know something that can help us. In fact, I know you do," I whispered while Grandma's back was turned, narrowing my eyes at him. It was hard to give a menacing look to someone who was wearing sunglasses, I noted.

He scowled at me and sighed. "I just want to live the rest of my life in peace, is that too much to ask?

Why won't everyone leave me alone? I found a nice woman," Grandma blushed at this, "and we have this nice place here. I just want to be left alone!" he said, throwing his hands up.

Zeb spoke up. "Why won't people leave you alone? What is it you do for a living, Gus?"

Gus glanced in Grandma's direction. "Betty, would you be a lamb and get my other glasses from the bedside table for me?" he asked her, clearly to get her out of the room for a few moments.

Grandma beamed. "Oh yes, I'll be right back!" She sashayed out of the room, the word "juicy" swinging back and forth as she went. I shook my head and made a mental note to take Grandma shopping for a new wardrobe soon.

When she was gone, Gus to turned to us and leaned in, lowering his gruff voice. "I'm a warlock, alright? People want spells and curses and then they wanna reverse 'em when things don't go their way," he rolled his eyes before continuing. "It's maddening and I've had enough. I just finished my last job. That's it for me, I'm done. So, whatever you think I can do for you, I can't." He sat back, crossing his arms once again.

"What was your last job? Was it for Robbie, who was just here? Please Gus, I'm begging you. My daughter, Mac—Betty's great-granddaughter—is in trouble," I said, hoping to appeal to his feelings for Grandma with that last bit.

He sighed. "Fine. Years ago, I worked a curse for a guy. I guess it was finally activated, and the accursed wanted me to lift it. It took me awhile. Hell, I made that curse a long time ago. But he paid well, so it was worth it," he said, and leaned forward before continuing. "I'm done, I made a killing off it, and I'm set for the rest of my life, however long that may be." He mimicked washing his hands and sat back in the chair.

"You cast the original curse for Edward Lambert? And you successfully lifted it? That's what we need!" I exclaimed, grinning and looking at Zeb. He didn't look as enthusiastic as I did.

"I'm still looking for your glasses, Sugar Britches, they weren't on the bedside table!" Grandma called from another room.

Gus sighed once again. "You don't get it, do you? One curse, one reversal. I know, there were two people involved in the original curse, so unless they cast the reversal together—" he stopped and shrugged.

It took me a moment to realize what he meant. The reversal was good for one use only and after what we'd seen from Aaron, he wouldn't be inviting Nina over for a curse lifting party.

"Shit," I said, putting my head in my hands. I looked up and said, "Can't you just make another one? Isn't there anything you can do?" Tears welled in my eyes, threatening to fall. Zeb took my hand and squeezed.

"Look, honey, I would if I could. You seem like a nice kid and all. The reversal called for a rare and specific ingredient and I don't have any more of it. I received just enough to make the one reversal, that's it," Gus said.

Zeb looked intrigued. "You received it? How so? Maybe we can get more?" he wondered.

We heard a crash from the other room and Grandma called, "I'm okay! Still looking!" Gus rolled his eyes.

"It was the strangest thing, really. The old guy, Edward, who I made the curse for years ago. I got a package from him through Robbie. He asked me to send a potion that would end his life, which would enact the curse. Normally, I would've chucked something like that in the garbage, but there was a bundle of cash in there that made it worth my while," he said, with a slight grin as one eyebrow rose over the dark sunglasses.

"Afterwards, I found a tiny vial of Snowdonia Hawkweed in the envelope. How he knew I'd need it for the reversal, I'm not sure. It was almost like he was asking me to lift the curse after he was dead. So, when Lambert's son asked me for the reversal, through Robbie, I went ahead with it," he said, throwing his hands up in the air before continuing. "I figured after all the cash the old guy paid me, it was the least I could do for him," Gus said.

Maybe Gus wasn't such a terrible guy after all, I thought.

He shrugged. "Anyway," he continued, "Snowdonia Hawkweed is one of the rarest plants in the world. I don't know how Lambert got his hands on it, but you can't just order it on Amazon." He gave me a brief look of regret at that.

Zeb rose from the table and said, "Right. So, we have to get the reversal from Robbie before he delivers it to Aaron." He pulled his phone out to look at the tracker he had installed on Robbie's vehicle. "We'd better hurry," he said to me.

"One more thing," Gus said, standing to follow us to the door. "You've probably figured it out by now, but you have a gift, Cricket," he said, which stopped me in my tracks.

"What? How do you know—" I began, but he cut me off.

"I knew the first day I met you when you came here to visit Betty. I'm not sure, but I think being around the vampires so much probably triggered it. Betty told me you work for Sunshine Cleaners. Everybody knows they're vampires," he added with a shrug.

"What else do you know about Revealers?" I asked, eager to know more about my newfound abilities.

He smiled, and it appeared to be genuine. "Come see me after you get your kid back."

I nodded at him. Zeb was waiting by the door, motioning for me to hurry.

"Grandma, we're going. I'll call you!" I yelled as I turned to follow Zeb out the door. I stopped and turned back to Gus before exiting the apartment.

"By the way, what's with the sunglasses?" I asked him.

He laughed at that and said, "That's a question for another day." With that, he closed the door after us, and we were on our way.

Chapter 23

We caught up to Robbie as he was pulling into the driveway at Aaron's house. Zeb pulled the car in behind him and we both got out. Robbie turned to stare at us in confusion. I noticed he had a vial in his hand.

Recognition soon dawned on his face as he realized who I was, and he made a run for the house. Zeb caught up to him and grabbed his arm, but not before Robbie said a few words in what sounded like Latin. I saw purple sparks flying about as Zeb pulled his hand back, gasping in pain.

Aaron emerged from the house, looking haggard and gaunt. "What's going on?" he asked. His face was pale and merely standing upright was taking a toll on him. I supposed he was having the same symptoms as Nina now that he was mortal.

"I have it!" Robbie yelled, waving the vial in the air and moving towards Aaron.

"Wait, please!" I said, running in their direction. "Please, Aaron, you can save Nina too!"

He smirked at me as I grew closer. "Why in hell would I want to save that bitch?" he asked. Robbie handed over the vial and Aaron held it up to the light, admiring the aquamarine color of the liquid.

"I know, I know. She's a bitch. But she's dying, just like you are. And she's holding my daughter hostage until I find out how to lift the curse," I said. I moved to close the distance between Aaron and I, hoping I might get close enough to grab the vial from his hand. He must have realized this and quickly stuck the vial in a pocket of his robe.

"She deserves to die for what she did to my father, then to me. She took advantage of him for his money, refused to divorce him even when things went south for them," he said, coughing into a handkerchief.

I stifled a sigh and stood with hands on hips, waiting for him to finish. I really didn't care what she had or hadn't done, I just wanted my daughter back. Zeb was still being held at a distance by Robbie and the implied threat of more magic being thrown at him.

"Didn't you want to be turned, though?" I said, hoping to distract him so I could figure out a way to get the damn vial.

When he finished his coughing spell, Aaron continued. "I was young, I didn't know what I wanted out of life back then. But did Nina care about that? No, she saw a way to hold on to the money even after my father died. She made me believe I wanted to be turned. She kept me away from my human friends or anyone else who might convince me otherwise," he said, narrowing his eyes and staring into the distance.

"And when my father found out our plans, he forbade her to turn me. She wouldn't listen to him, she did it anyway. Had me utterly convinced that she loved me and that becoming a vampire was the only way we could be together," he said. He sagged a little as he spoke, as if it was all an enormous weight he had been carrying around.

I made a move towards him, and he held up one hand to keep me back. I glanced at Zeb, who shrugged.

"I spoke to my dad a few weeks ago, behind her back. I've been doing a lot of things behind her back for quite some time now," he added with a slight smile, risking a glance at Robbie. "He forgave me, and he promised that if Robbie and I helped him get what he needed to end his life and activate the curse that he would make it so I could be saved. But not her. Never her," he finished, nearly spitting that last bit.

"Please, Aaron. I don't care what happens to her after, I just need her to let my daughter go," I said, resorting to outright begging. I could feel tears welling up, ready to spill down my cheeks.

Aaron looked at me for a few moments. His hand went to the robe pocket that held the vial and after a moment's consideration, he frowned. "I'm sorry. I just can't," he said, and turned to go back inside the house. Robbie saw this and hurried to follow, with Zeb and I in their wake. Zeb caught the door before it closed, and we followed them inside.

"Robbie, how do I do this?" Aaron asked, taking the vial out and examining it once again. He didn't seem to care that we had followed them inside, he acted as if he didn't even see us anymore.

"Drink it, then I'll say the words the old man told me. That will activate it," Robbie said. His face grew serious, and he continued, "But first, my money."

Aaron rolled his eyes with some effort. "You'll get your money, lover boy. Do you not trust me?" he said in an exasperated tone.

Robbie's mouth turned up in a grin. "I love you, but no, I don't trust you," he said. "So, how much more time do you want to waste? Unlike you, I have plenty of it," he continued, leaning against the wall with a smirk.

"It's that attitude that I love to hate about you," Aaron said with a sly grin. "Bedside table, top drawer. Hurry back," he said, nodding his head towards the stairs. Robbie took off, leaving us alone with Aaron.

"You're doing this? Leaving her out of the reversal and letting her die? Didn't she ever mean anything to you at all?" I said in a last-ditch effort to convince him or at least make him hesitate and buy us a little time.

Realizing we were still in the room with him, he turned to me, startled. "Yes, I am doing this without her. So, you can see yourselves out now," Aaron said, gesturing to the door.

I looked at Zeb, who stepped towards Aaron. "Mate, isn't there anything—" he started, but Aaron cut him off.

"I said NOW!" Aaron yelled. I jumped, not expecting someone literally at death's door to yell with such vehemence.

"Alright, alright. Cricket," Zeb said, then motioned for me to follow him to the door. We would have to figure something else out and quick. My stomach was in knots and I felt like I could vomit all over Aaron's posh carpet.

Zeb opened the door and there stood Nina, with Chad next to her.

She was a shell of her old self, hunched over and clutching a bloody handkerchief to her mouth. Her skin was nearly translucent, her hair was thin and had gone completely white. No longer the young, confident leader of the Ministry of Vampire Affairs, she was now a shrunken old woman, not long for this world.

I gasped upon seeing her, and then Chad pushed past us, pulling her along behind him.

Zeb whispered to me, "She doesn't have long, I can feel it. She has much less time than he does, maybe only a matter of minutes." He pushed his sleeve up and showed me part of his tattoo that was turning from black to red. I made a mental note to circle back to the tattoo thing after all of this was over with.

"Aaron, my love," Nina said as she approached him slowly. Aaron's eyes grew wide upon seeing her, and he backed away.

"Robbie!" he yelled, which brought on another coughing fit. Nina seemed unaffected and moved to embrace him, which he avoided.

"I'm here now, love. We can lift the curse and run away together. It's what we always wanted, and now it can be reality. At last," Nina whispered, her voice hoarse with the effort.

Aaron looked at her in disbelief. "How many times do I have to tell you it's over for us? That you ruined my life and my father's life, too. I don't want to be with you anymore," he said. He scowled at her and continued, "I won't share the reversal spell with you. It's time you paid for what you did to us."

Robbie came back down the stairs, shoving a wad of bills into his jacket pocket on his way. Immediately upon seeing Nina and Chad, he went into attack mode. He raised his hands and said some words which sounded like a mixture of Greek and Latin to me, and Nina shrieked, covering her ears. Chad grabbed his ears also and howled, doubling over.

"Stop!" Aaron yelled and Robbie ceased his chanting. Nina and Chad recovered themselves from whatever magic Robbie had thrown at them. I was thankful to have been left out of it, whatever it was.

Aaron leveled his gaze at Nina and after a moment, he said, "She's leaving." He turned from us and walked into the unlit living room.

Nina collapsed to the floor, sobbing. "Aaron! Aaron! Don't you understand, I did it all because I love you! I love you!" she wailed. Chad sat next to her, cradling her limp body as her cries softened.

Robbie moved towards them, but Zeb put up a hand. He kneeled next to Nina and gently placed his hand on her cheek. He looked at me and shook his head. I gasped, and my hand flew to my mouth.

"She's gone?" I asked, knowing the answer.

Zeb nodded. "She's gone," he confirmed.

Chad wept at that, rocking Nina's lifeless body as he sat holding her in Aaron's foyer. Robbie nodded at us and turned to follow Aaron into the next room, where presumably they would invoke the reversal curse and save Aaron's life.

I crumpled to the floor also, not sure what all of this meant for Mac. Where was she? Did Nina leave instructions with Chad to kill her in the event of her final death? Was she already dead?

I sobbed, hugging myself and rocking. I had no idea what to do now. I went on like that for what seemed like several minutes, then I heard something I thought I might never hear again.

"Mom?" Mac said with a strangled sob, running towards me. Was I hallucinating? Could it possibly be Mac, free from Nina's grasp finally? I saw Zeb standing at the door behind her, smiling from ear to ear.

"Look who I found, Princess," he said as Mac slid to the floor and pulled me into a hug. I hugged her back so hard I thought I might break her ribs. I began to cry again, but they were tears of joy now. She was crying too and laughing.

"Mackenzie Grace! I thought I'd lost you forever! I'm so sorry, I'm so sorry," I murmured in her ear between sobs.

"It's okay, Mom, I'm here now. It's over and I'm okay. Alright?" Mac said, stroking my hair. I pulled back a bit to look at her. I had to make sure she was indeed okay. She wore her long black hair scraped back into a messy ponytail. She wore black jeans with rips in the knees, which were most likely there before her ordeal began. A black hoodie that looked only a little dirty completed her look, and I was thankful she didn't look much worse for wear.

"Are you sure you're okay? Did they hurt you? Did Chad…" I asked, trailing off with that last bit, not wanting to think about what Chad could've done to her.

"Chad was a douchebag, but no, he didn't hurt me. Neither did she," Mac said, nodding towards Nina's body. Chad still sat holding her, silent now and staring off into space. "They didn't have anything vegan for me to eat though," Mac said, rolling her eyes.

I burst out laughing. Yeah, she was fine. She was absolutely fine. I pulled her into another hug and planted kisses all over her forehead and cheeks while she yelled for me to stop.

Zeb laughed as I tortured her with affection. After we calmed down a bit, we got up from the floor and made our way into Aaron's kitchen. He and Robbie seemed to have abandoned us, so there was no urgent need to leave, I figured.

As we made our way there, Zeb pulled me back for a moment. "I need to deal with… them," he said, indicating Nina and Chad. "Can you birds wait in the kitchen 'til I'm done?" he asked, flashing that smile I hadn't seen in so many days.

It was obvious I wasn't the only one feeling relieved. I was thrilled to have Mac back, but I wasn't sure how to feel about Nina. I hated her, yes, but did I want her dead? I'd need time to process and reflect, I decided. But not today.

I reached up, wrapping my arms around his neck, pulling him closer. "I guess we can do that," I said. I smiled at him and went in for a kiss. He kissed me back, and I swear, I saw fireworks. Red, blue, green, silver. Every color fireworks come in. I gave his lower lip a little nip with my teeth and he growled a bit, kissing me again.

"Ewww. God, can't we even get home first?" Mac said from the kitchen doorway, a look of disgust on her pretty face as she rolled her eyes at us. She had a can of soda in one hand and a bag of chips in the other. So much for veganism. She spun on her heel and went back to the kitchen.

I glanced at Zeb and that's all it took. We both began giggling uncontrollably. I leaned into him and laughed into his shoulder as he planted another kiss on the top of my head.

"Alright, alright. I'll be quick as I can, then I'll take you lot home," Zeb said, giving my hand a squeeze as we both collected ourselves. He turned to do his job and collect the soul of the deceased. That's interesting, I thought. Vampires have souls, who knew?

I started for the kitchen and thought maybe I should check in on Aaron and Robbie first. I made my way to the dark living room where I'd seen them both disappear to previously. It was still dark and quiet. And empty. I flipped the light switch on and saw the vial lying on the floor, also empty. I glanced out the window and saw Robbie's black sedan was missing. It seemed they had vanished.

I retraced my steps and headed for the kitchen to join Mac and wait for Zeb to finish up with Nina so we could go home.

Chapter 24

We arrived back at the duplex a couple hours later. Mac complained of an upset stomach, probably from the recent transition from vegan to junk food. I checked her over again, just to make sure she was alright, and sent her up to bed where she planned to call Luther and go to sleep.

Zeb sat on my couch, leaned back with one ankle resting on the opposite knee. His arm stretched across the back of the couch and he gave me a smoldering look that said, "get your ass over here right now". So I obliged.

I sat next to him, fitting myself into the curve of his arm which he dropped from the couch to rest on my shoulder, pulling me close. I rested my head on his chest and felt his heart beating fast and hard.

He put a finger under my chin and tilted my head up, looking me in the eye for a moment. Those sparkling blue eyes set the butterflies in my stomach into flight. He closed his eyes and pressed his lips to mine gently. I kissed him back, softly at first, then with increasing urgency.

Realizing where we were and that a self-righteous, judgmental teenager was upstairs, who may or may not be asleep yet, I pulled back from his kiss and said, "Maybe we should take this to your place?"

Zeb grinned. "I thought you'd never ask," he said. He rose from the couch, catching my hand and tangling his fingers together with mine. He pulled me up, and we practically ran out the door and into his side of the duplex.

We giggled like teenagers as he unlocked his door and pulled me inside. The door was barely closed behind us before he had his hands in my hair, pulling me to him, kissing me, over and over and over. My hands roamed over his broad chest, his muscular arms, down to the waistband of his jeans. Zeb's hands went to the hem of my t-shirt and he dragged it over my head, revealing the black lace bra I was wearing. He pulled back momentarily, looking at me appreciatively with a cheeky grin.

"Lovely, Princess," he said, pulling me in for another kiss. "I almost hate to take it off you," he whispered, one hand grappling at my back with the bra clasp. After a moment, he had it unfastened, and he tossed it to the living room floor. He pulled me close again, one hand cupping a breast while the other ran through my long blonde hair. He kissed me again, and I gently bit his lower lip, eliciting a growl from him. I smiled against his mouth, and we made our way to the couch.

My hands went to the front of his jeans and I unbuttoned them and worked the zipper down, feeling how hard he was through the fabric. We fell to the couch. He finished removing the jeans and the boxer briefs he had been wearing. I wound up lying on top of him on the couch while we continued kissing and groping.

Zeb helped me wriggle out of my jeans and the black lace panties that matched my bra. He tossed them both aside, and the jeans ended up slung over the television while the panties landed on his black leather boots. I giggled and pulled his t-shirt over his head, then added it to the collection on the floor.

We lay together, skin on skin, exploring each other's bodies. He cupped my face and kissed me, long and hard. I kissed him back while my hands wandered over his body, finding his hard length and making him gasp as I stroked him. He moaned and whispered, "Cricket."

Then he rolled on top of me, kissing me with urgency. He trailed kisses down the side of my neck and made his way to my breasts. While one hand caressed a breast, he kissed the other, his tongue darting out to tease my nipple. I arched my back and moaned; I was so ready. I wanted him now. "Zeb, please." I breathed.

He looked up at me, clearly pleased. He moved to the other breast, giving it the same treatment, which left me squirming and twisting with desire.

One firm hand made its way to my core, and I gasped when I felt his fingers slide inside me. I spread my legs wider in invitation and moaned his name. After a few thrusts, he growled and returned to kiss my lips. His hands slid under my ass, lifting me until we were both in a sitting position. I straddled him on the couch, my thighs over his and my legs stretched out behind him on the couch.

Zeb took my face in his hands and gently kissed me, his thumbs tracing my cheekbones. I ran my nails lightly down his back, feeling him shiver as I did. He combed his fingers through my hair and pulled back to look at me. His blue eyes smoldered, melting me into a puddle of desire.

"Cricket," he whispered. Without breaking eye-contact, he grasped my hips and pulled me close, thrusting into me.

He moved slowly at first, holding me close to him, kissing my neck and breasts while we found a rhythm. I threw my head back, savoring the feeling of him inside me, thrusting deeper and faster. I moved to meet him every time, welcoming the sensations that had us both gasping and moaning.

In a fluid motion, Zeb wrapped an arm around my waist and shifted us until I was lying on my back with him above me. He entered me again, thrusting deeper and harder as I wrapped my legs around his hips and my arms around his neck, drawing him down to my lips. I kissed him hard as I felt the pressure within me building until it was almost unbearable. I dragged my nails down his back, which made him groan as he kissed my collarbone.

I closed my eyes, seeing all the colors of the rainbow behind my eyelids, bursting like fireworks. Zeb said my name in a low rumble, and I shattered into a million pieces as he rocked against me, harder and faster. Zeb buried his face in my hair and held me close as he withdrew just in time.

He collapsed, and I shifted so he was lying next to me on the large couch. I slung one leg over his and rested my head on his heaving chest. We both caught our breath and collected ourselves, while Zeb played with my hair. After I'd recovered a bit, a random thought struck me, and I laughed. Zeb caught my chin with his other hand and tilted my head up, his eyebrows raised.

"Laughter is not exactly the reaction I was going for, Princess," he said with a grin as I giggled again.

"I just thought—" I started, doing my best to stifle the laughter long enough to tell him. "I'll bet

Grandma's couch has never seen that much action before," I finished and allowed the giggles to escape.

I felt Zeb's chest shake with laughter and he said, "Oh, I don't know about that, did you see your Nan with that geezer, Gus? I'll bet they do some proper snogging," he said, laughing as I punched his arm.

"Ewww! Well at least it wasn't on this particular couch," I said, trying to erase the mental picture of Grandma and Gus together like that. Gross.

The laughter subsided, and we continued to lie there. I gently traced the tattoos on his arm. "When are you going to tell me more about yourself, Mr. Reaper?" I said in a playful tone. I felt his muscles tense up at that.

He grew serious and with a sigh said, "I will. I promise, but not tonight. I don't want to ruin this," he said, stroking my cheek and pushing a stray hair behind my ear.

"How could telling me about your past ruin anything?" I asked, continuing to trace the intricate black line work designs on his arm.

"They don't make just anyone a Reaper, Cricket. I did something a long time ago. That's what's got me into this mess and I'm trying my best to fix it," he said, running one hand through his blond hair. "I don't want it to change how you think of me," he said, staring at me intently.

I raised up on an elbow to look at him. "Are you kidding me? There's nothing you could say that would change my opinion of you. You went out of your way to help me save my daughter. You've kept me safe the past few weeks when I didn't even know I was in danger. Although you stalked me and use questionable tactics," I added, narrowing my eyes and nudging him playfully, which made him smile.

"Seriously, that tells me everything I need to know about what kind of person you are. Whatever you did, however bad it was, I don't think you're that man now. How could you be?" I asked, bringing my hand to cup his cheek. I leaned in to kiss him softly.

"Cricket—" he began with a shake of his head before I cut him off.

"Hey, no pressure, you can tell me whenever you're ready," I added, seeing relief flood into his blue eyes.

He pulled me down to him again and held me close. He planted a kiss on top of my head. "Thank you for saying that. I *will* tell you, I promise. Just let me find my way of doing it. I hope you'll still feel that way—" I cut him off with another kiss.

Chapter 25

I was enjoying my third cup of coffee, lounging around the house in sweatpants and a hoodie with my hair in a messy bun when the doorbell rang. I was on the couch with my feet up on the coffee table, texting Doreen while Chip and Joanna talked about wainscoting on television. Zeb? Probably not, I thought. We had parted late last night. Or early this morning, however you wanted to look at it. And he'd said he had work to do today. I wasn't expecting anyone else. Curious, I sat my coffee and the phone down and went to answer the door.

"What the hell are you doing here?" I asked upon opening the door and seeing Chad standing there, looking chagrined.

I went to slam the door in his face, but he caught it and said, "Please, Cricket. Just give me five minutes, I promise I'm not here to start any shit." He looked haggard and run down. Like he had no reason to go on. He must have really cared about Nina, I thought, and despite my better judgment I opened the door and stepped out onto the porch. I wouldn't let him in, I wasn't that crazy.

I crossed my arms and gave him an icy stare. "I'll give you three minutes, and they start now," I said.

"Look, I don't blame you if you hate me. I just wanted to return this." He held out a tube of lipstick. I took it and saw "Unicorn Blood" on the label. I stuck it in my pocket without responding and looked at him again with my best Resting Bitch Face.

"And give you this," he continued, fumbling for an envelope in his jacket pocket. He handed it to me and said, "Nina wasn't an evil person, you know."

I rolled my eyes.

"She felt bad about what she did to you and Mac, that's why she had me take her to Aaron's. She figured you were there, and she wanted to return Mac to you and try to convince Aaron to help her on her own. She ran out of time before she could say any of that to you," he said, looking down at the envelope in his hands.

I huffed, ready for him to go away so I could go back to Chip and Joanna.

"I figured telling you now was the least I could do for her," Chad continued, ignoring my impatience. His eyes were red and glistening. Shit, had he been in love with her? I thought, taking the envelope from him and shoving it into my pocket with the lipstick.

"I don't know what you want me to say. She kidnapped my daughter."

The truth was, I sort of believed him. I had worked for the woman and been in her house, after all. I didn't think she was truly evil. I believed she was desperate and made a lot of poor decisions, though. Decisions that could've hurt or even killed my daughter. And that is what I could not bring myself to forgive her for.

He visibly sagged, maybe with relief at getting it off his chest. "I understand. I just thought you should know. Also, she wanted you to have the envelope," he said, turning to leave, then facing me once again.

"Oh, and just so you know, I'm going to turn myself in to the Ministry right now for my part in this," he added, then started down the front porch stairs.

I watched him go and went inside to call Carl. I got his voice mail, so I briefly described last night's events, although he probably already knew, and told him about Chad's visit and that he was supposedly on his way to the Ministry to turn himself in. I also asked him to call me so we could talk about my position with the Ministry, considering the recent developments.

I sat down and pulled the envelope out of my pocket, along with the lipstick. I would give that to Mac later, if she even wanted it.

What could be in here that Nina wanted me to have? I thought, running a finger under the seal to open it. I pulled out a few pages and my mouth dropped open as I read.

It was a will, or what passed as a will for an undead person. I continued reading and found that she had left her entire estate to Mac, under my guardianship, until she turned twenty-one. She'd also provided a college fund, which was more than enough for Mac to get a degree at MIT, or any other higher education institution that she could possibly want to attend.

I dropped the paperwork to the table and covered my eyes, resting my elbows on my knees. I cried; I couldn't help it.

Damn her, I thought. Why did she have to go and do that? I'd have to sort this out later with Carl and would probably have to hire my own lawyer too. Damn it, Nina, I thought again, fresh tears spilling from my eyes.

My phone rang, trilling "The Vampire Club" by Aurelio Voltaire, so I answered it without even looking at the caller ID. It was Carl's ringtone.

"Hello," I said, wiping my eyes and trying to gather myself.

It was his secretary instead who said, "Hi Cricket, can you come in tonight for a meeting with Carl?"

I said I could, and we agreed on eight p.m. at Sunshine Cleaners. I knew he would want the scoop on what happened with Nina and we would need to talk about what her final death would mean for my position at the Ministry.

I had some time to kill before my meeting with Carl, so I thought I'd swing by Forever Young and fill Grandma in and let her know that Mac was okay. I'm sure we gave her a scare when we were chasing Robbie, which led us to her and Gus's place at the senior center.

As soon as I walked in the door, I spotted Grandma holding court in the rec room. She was teaching a bunch of other old ladies how to floss. And I don't mean what you do to your teeth. They were all gyrating their hips and moving their arms back and forth while Grandma cheered them on.

"That's it, Mildred! You've got it!" Grandma yelled to one of the ladies. I closed my eyes and pinched the bridge of my nose as she spotted me.

"Come dance with us, Cricket!" Grandma said as she flossed her way over to me. She hugged me and then turned to the ladies. "Keep practicing, girls!"

She steered me to a small table with two chairs in the corner of the rec room. We sat, and she grasped my hands across the table.

"How is Mac? How are you? What happened?" Gone was the happy-go-lucky floss instructor of two minutes ago. Now she just wanted to know that her granddaughters were okay.

I squeezed her hands. "Mac is fine and I'm fine. After we caught up to Robbie, things didn't quite go as expected, but it all worked out. I wanted to say I'm sorry for dragging you into all of this and for worrying you. But Mac and I are fine, so you don't have to worry about us anymore." I smiled at her. She frowned and pulled her hands out of mine.

"That's it?" she said, with a frown.

"What do you mean, 'that's it'? Aren't you happy we're okay?" I asked, incredulously. She's lucky we're related, I thought, mentally rolling my eyes.

She sighed and threw her hands up in the air. "You're okay? That's all I get? No details? Gus won't say a word either. I swear, if I didn't know better, I'd think you all were keeping something from me." She crossed her arms over her chest and continued to glare.

Alright, I'm gonna have to get her off of this subject before I wind up telling her I'm a Revealer and that vampires, werewolves, and witches exist and that she's engaged to one of the above.

"Fine. Zeb and I may, sort of, possibly, be a thing now," I said, pursing my lips together to keep from grinning from ear to ear. I knew this would completely derail her train of thought and well, the thought of being a "thing" with Zeb actually made me happy.

215

As expected, Grandma's eyes lit up and she squealed, putting her hands to her mouth. "Cricket! Oh, I'm so happy for you! That Zeb is a real catch. Did you see his buns in those tight jeans he wears?" She giggled.

I laughed too. "Yeah Grandma, I did. But what are you doing looking at Zeb's buns?" I asked playfully.

"Well, sometimes a girl just can't help herself, you know," Grandma said. She rose from her seat and hugged me tight, still laughing. "I'd better get back to the ladies and our dance lesson now, but I'm so glad you stopped by. And I am glad that my girls are okay. Very glad!" She kissed the top of my head before toddling off to continue her flossing lessons.

I shook my head, smiling and watching her go. Grandma Betty was something else. Gus sure has his hands full, God love him, I thought.

She turned around, as if reading my mind, and said, "Oh by the way, Gus wanted me to ask you and Mac over for dinner soon. He wants to get to know you girls better, isn't that cute?" she said and was off. Yes, and I want to get to know Gus better myself, along with everything he knows about Revealers and the supernatural world, I thought.

I was about to grab my bag and go when I got a text. I looked at my phone on my way through the parking lot of Forever Young.

Drinks on the porch 2nite?
It was from Zeb, and I smiled. I got in the car and typed out a reply.
Yes, will be late, mtg with Carl @8

Then I accidentally hit the eggplant emoji as I was hitting send. Great. Almost immediately, he sent back a smiling devil emoji. Then I sent a hand emoji with the middle finger extended, along with an eye roll emoji for good measure and threw my phone in my bag.

It was right at eight when I was walking into Sunshine Cleaners and the receptionist showed me into Carl's stark white office. He was tapping away on his keyboard, and barely looked up as I entered the room.

"Please, have a seat," the receptionist said, indicating the white chairs in front of Carl's desk. I nodded to her, took a seat, and waited for an acknowledgment.

After a few minutes of listening to him type, he finished up whatever he was doing. He looked up, appearing almost surprised to see me sitting there.

"Oh, Cricket, good. You're here."

"Yes, I am," I said, not knowing what else to say. Vampires are so weird, I thought.

He folded his hands beneath his chin and stared at me.

"Give me your take on what happened, then," he said. No pleasantries with this guy, I thought.

I took a deep breath and relayed everything that happened. Nina, Robbie, Aaron, Edward, the curse, the cure, the abduction of my daughter, all of it. I figured I might as well, he'll probably hear it all anyway if he doesn't know already and it would only make me look like I have something to hide if I hadn't told him everything. I even told him I know what I am—a Revealer.

Carl nodded his head, said "hmmm" in appropriate places, and wrote a couple of things down while I talked. When I reached the part about my newly discovered status as a supernatural radar detector, he put his pencil down and looked me dead in the eye.

"About that. Yes, we knew. It was one reason we wanted to bring you on, we knew that when the power manifested itself in you that you would become invaluable to us," he said, leaning back in his posh, white chair.

"We've been watching you for some time and when you got fired from your paralegal job, it was the perfect opportunity for us to hire you. Now that you have your powers, we need to renegotiate our relationship and expectations," Carl said, leveling his gaze at me.

I was still trying to process the fact that they knew before I did.

"You knew? How?"

Carl smiled, but it did not reach his eyes. "It doesn't matter right now. What matters is that you realize your capabilities and use them to their fullest potential. We can help you with that."

Since I barely knew what I was capable of at this point, besides feeling a little static electricity when I got within an arm's length of a supernatural being, he intrigued me. I wanted to know what he knew about my abilities.

I tilted my head and said, "How can you help, exactly?"

Carl smirked. "Cricket, do you think the vampire community picked Nashville out of the blue as a location in which to set up a Ministry office? No, they didn't. For reasons we are still trying to understand, the middle Tennessee area, mainly Nashville, has become a hotbed of supernatural activity within the last twenty-five years," he said, standing to walk the length of the room as he spoke.

"More and more 'supes', as we call ourselves, are relocating here. They say they feel led or pulled to this area, and we don't know why. So the Ministry put an office here, not only to govern the vampires in this area but also to determine the reason behind the influx of supes to this part of the country at such a rapid rate in such a brief period of time. We have our theories, but nothing solid yet," he explained, then stopped walking and turned to face me.

"We believe you can help us with your Revealer abilities. We would like you to work for us in that capacity instead of the prior arrangements we had made. Doreen will take over the DC department instead, leaving you free to develop your abilities and use them to help us. We will continue to compensate you well," he added. He sat forward, putting his elbows on his desk, to wait for my reply.

I wanted to learn more about this ability and how to use it. But did I want to use it for the MVA's benefit? Having so many supernatural beings in the area had to put humans at risk though, so maybe it would be worth it if I could potentially keep people safe?

There was so much to think about and learn, and I was only just breaking the surface. I needed help to figure this out and maybe Carl and the MVA were a means to that end? I took a deep breath.

"Okay, we have a deal. But I want access to everything. All the information you have about

Revealers and their abilities and everything you know about every supe out there."

Carl smiled. "You have my word," he said, extending his hand to shake mine.

I hesitated. "And if I want to quit working for you one day, what then?" I asked. Carl's smile faltered, but he recovered quickly.

"We would come to terms we could both agree upon to facilitate your exit from our employment at that point in time," he said, in a much colder voice. A bullshit answer, but it was as good as I would get.

"Put that in the contract. I guess we have a deal then," I said, grasping Carl's icy hand in mine to shake on it.

He beamed as we shook. "Perfect. I will have Alex draw up the paperwork and send it over for your signature tomorrow. I'll be in touch soon so we can begin," he said, releasing my hand. He opened the office door and ushered me out. That was that.

The meeting took less time than I had thought, which was good because I was excited to get home and share a drink with Zeb. So, I decided to put all thoughts about vampires, werewolves, and whatever else goes bump in the night, out of my head as I drove home.

Chapter 26

Zeb was sitting on the front porch step with a couple of beers when I got home. I made my way up the driveway and smiled at him. I already knew that Mac was at Luther's house, so we had the whole duplex to ourselves.

"Rough day, Princess?" he asked, holding out a beer to me. I accepted and took a drink as I sat down on the step next to him.

My thigh touched his as I did, and it made my stomach do little flips. What am I, a teenager with a crush on the high school quarterback? I thought and felt my cheeks flush. I hadn't felt this way since back in the early days of my relationship with Mac's dad, John-Clarke. I had to admit, it was nice.

I clinked my beer can against his and said, "Nah, not too bad. Got a new job at the Ministry. They want me to use my 'supe' radar for them." Zeb laughed and took my hand, tangling our fingers together.

After a few moments, he turned and looked deeply into my eyes, his expression growing serious. Oh no, I thought, as my stomach dropped.

"Cricket..." Zeb began while looking at our entwined fingers and stroking the back of my hand with his thumb.

"Something's wrong, isn't it?" I said, preparing myself for the worst. Was he going to say that he didn't feel the same way about me? That our night together was a mistake? That he has a wife and three kids in upstate New York? I had already started mentally berating myself for being stupid enough to trust him when he interrupted my thoughts.

221

He put an arm around me and drew me to him. "It's my work. Now that you are aware of your ability and will work in a greater capacity at the Ministry, you're officially off Death Inc.'s radar," he said with a sigh.

"In other words, they think you don't need my protection any longer. They're sending me somewhere else," he whispered that last part, his voice breaking up a bit.

I pulled back to look at him. "What? No! I still need you! And people die every day around here. Who do I need to call? Give me your boss's name and number right now," I said, moving back into his embrace. My head was against his chest, I could hear the beating of his heart and smell his aftershave. I didn't want him to go, not now when we were just getting started.

He stroked my hair and planted a kiss on the top of my head. "It's not that far, they're only sending me to Atlanta for a bit. Something about a crazed kangaroo shifter who kicked several people to death. It wasn't their time yet, so somebody has to go deal with it and apprehend him," Zeb explained, still stroking my hair and my back.

"You're joking, right?" I asked with a laugh.

He cut his eyes at me and shrugged, grinning.

"Wait, there are kangaroo shifters?"

Zeb laughed. "If you can name it, there's someone out there who can shift into it," he said.

"Unicorns? Bears? Dragons? How about hamsters?" I said, rattling off the first things I could think of. Surely there weren't hamster shifters, I thought, giggling out loud.

"Yes, yes, yes, and unfortunately for them, yes," Zeb said, laughing with me.

When our giggles finally subsided, I took another drink from my beer.

"Damn it, Zeb. I don't want you to go," I said, leaning my head against his shoulder.

He sighed. "Believe me, I don't want to go either. I don't have a choice though," he said, his left hand absently touching his right arm where his tattoo sleeve was. "I'll keep paying your Nan rent because I hope to be back in a couple months. And I can't have some other bloke renting it from her and stealing you away from me, can I?"

I punched his arm, making him laugh. "You make it sound like I'd date anyone who lived next door!" I said with mock outrage.

With a grin, he pulled me to him again, wrapping his muscular arms around me.

"I'll miss you, Cricket," he said, as he tilted my chin up and kissed me softly. He cupped my face with one hand and kissed me again. My arms went around his neck, and I ran my hands through his spiky blond hair. Just when I had gotten used to him being around, he was leaving. It wasn't fair.

He rested his forehead against mine, still holding me close. "I might miss you a little bit too," I breathed.

He laughed, and my cell phone buzzed with a text message. I pulled it out of my bag and read.

Time for your first assignment, we'll get to your training as we can. Something important has come up. There's a lone werewolf in town and we need to find out why he's here. I think you're familiar with him already. Joseph Morley.

I read the text and went cold. I had an assignment already. And it was Joey?

"Alright, Princess?" Zeb asked, noticing the sudden change in my demeanor after reading the text from Carl.

I decided I didn't want to ruin tonight by obsessing and worrying over it. Who knows, it could even be the last night we have together before Zeb has to leave. So, I faced Zeb with a smile.

"I'm fine. That's tomorrow's problem," I said, tossing the cell phone into my bag.

I grabbed his flannel shirt and pulled him close to me, kissing him deeply. I'd worry about Joey Morley and Carl in the morning. Tonight, I had other things to do.

About the Author

Shauna is a paranormal romance author who aspires to become a professional time traveler. Bitter End (book one of the Nashville Immortals series), is her first novel. She's currently hard at work on book two, as well as short stories for several anthologies. She writes about all things paranormal and lives vicariously through her characters.

Shauna lives near Nashville, TN with her husband, son, their dog, and a beta fish. She loves books, coffee, wine, and bacon, in no particular order.

www.shaunajaredauthor.com
instagram.com/shaunajaredauthor/
facebook.com/shaunajaredauthor
twitter.com/shaunajared

Printed in Great Britain
by Amazon